TEXAS
Wesleyan
U N I V E R S I T Y

Eric in the Land of the Insects

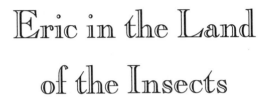

Eric in the Land of the Insects

Godfried Bomans

Translated from the Dutch by
Regina Louise Kornblith

Illustrated by
Mark Richardson

HOUGHTON MIFFLIN COMPANY
BOSTON 1994

Copyright © 1941 by Het Spectrum BV
First American edition 1994
Originally published in the Netherlands in 1941 by Het Spectrum BV
English translation copyright © 1994 by Gina Louise Sanders
Illustrations copyright © 1994 by Mark Richardson

Library of Congress Cataloging-in-Publication Data

Bomans, Godfried, 1917–1971.
    Eric in the land of the insects / by Godfried Bomans ; translated
from the Dutch by Regina Louise Kornblith. — 1st American ed.
        p.   cm.
    Summary: Nine-year-old Eric enters a landscape painting on his
bedroom wall and discovers a world of meadow insects startlingly
similar to his own world.
    ISBN 0–395–65231–6
    [1. Fantasy.   2. Insects—Fiction.]   I. Title.
PZ7.B6364Er   1994   93–24071
[Fic]—dc20   CIP
                              AC

Printed in the United States of America

VB   10   9   8   7   6   5   4   3   2   1

To MWA, for whom I learned
the language, and from whom
I have learned so much else

— R.L.K.

"Noi tutti siamo esiliati, viventi
entro le cornici di uno strano quadro.
Chi sa questo, vive da grande.
Gli altri sono insetti."

"We are all exiles, living within
the frame of a strange painting.
He who knows this, lives greatly.
All others are insects."

— Leonardo da Vinci
(in a letter to Gabriele Piccolomini)

Eric in the Land of the Insects

CHAPTER ONE

At the moment this story begins, we find young Eric lying in Grandmother Pinksterblom's old canopy bed under the patchwork quilt, staring out over the edge of the white sheets into the darkening room. It is the time when young children have just gone to bed, the time that grownups know nothing about. All the old familiar things on the wall fade gently into the growing darkness and the world becomes still — so still that it seems to have stopped breathing. Outside, someone walks past; slap, slap, sound the footsteps. And in the distance the high, shrill voice of an older child calls to a friend. The sound echoes in the evening air and you think: there are still some lucky ones about who don't yet have to be in bed.

Eric lay still and looked toward the window in the distance and at the dusty portraits on the walls. It always seems as though something is going to happen, he thought. Perhaps tonight is the night! And he decided that he would try very hard not to fall asleep right away, as he did on other evenings, but to stay awake and pay careful attention to see whether or not indeed something *would* happen. And he had a perfect method for keeping awake. Under his pillow lay a small book, *Solm's Concise Natural History.* Tomorrow afternoon in school there would be a test on all the insects described in it. He had spent most of the day studying and was up to the mayflies. He planned to finish it up in the morning during recess.

"Let's see," mumbled Eric, "how many legs does a wasp have? Six. The eyes focus separately and are placed forward on the head. Good! They don't live in hives like bees, but — oh, where *do* they live? They must live alone, I guess. But it doesn't matter. They belong to the Hymenoptera family and have moveable antennae. And what about butterflies? 'The butterfly surprises the attentive naturalist with its bright display of color. (Eric repeated this sentence twice — he found it so delightful.) We classify them among the so-called useful insects, but their offspring, called caterpillars, are capable of much damage. The articulated, moveable head (and now came a long tiresome passage that had caused Eric much difficulty) is adorned with multiple stiff, brushlike, often twisted, saw-toothed or comb-shaped bristles, protruding semiglobular simple eyes, a small upper jaw, and an extensible tongue, which takes the place of the lower jaw.' Now — that's that! And I bet Willy Martin couldn't do it better!"

Willy Martin was the smartest boy in the third grade and he sat a few seats in front of Eric.

"And now the ants." (Eric liked the ants, mainly because most of the entry was in small print, which was not required reading in his class.) " 'The ant, like the wasp, belongs to the Hymenoptera family. Ants are frequently held up as good examples to people, and not without reason—they are diligent creatures. They live together in great numbers in so-called anthills,' (that's easy to remember, thought Eric, ants, anthills) 'where they are always busy with one thing and another. When threatened, they exude an acid—called ant acid—which is very caustic. The males, called drones, are born in the late summer. They have wings, but they lack the stinger of the females and the workers.' That's strange, thought Eric. One would have expected just the opposite. Let's have a look.

He withdrew *Solm's Concise Natural History* from under his pillow and opened it to the chapter on the ants. And, indeed, there it was: "but they lack the stinger of the females and the workers." "That is very strange," muttered Eric. "What kind of males can they be?" He glanced at the painting that hung on the wall next to his bed—*Industrious Valley*. The painting actually had no title of its own, but Eric himself had baptized it *Industrious Valley* because of the prodigious activity of the portrayed inhabitants. It is true that a few fluffy, white sheep were grazing peacefully in the green distance, and the old shepherd who tended them

3

was leaning restfully on his staff while a younger one lazily played the flute. But the part of the picture that Eric liked best was the foreground, where the artist had painted every possible insect that one could think of in exquisite detail and with endless patience. Here all were diligently at work: caterpillars and beetles crept along branches seeking food; tiny spiders wove their webs; fat honeybees were busy among the flowers. Right next to the bottom of the frame was a huge snail shell. It must be so big because it's so close, thought Eric. In the grass in the lower right, a worm wriggled in what seemed to be both directions at once and a grave-digger beetle stood nearby watching with interest, as though he wondered which end was going to win the tug of war. There were ants, too, racing hurriedly past each other through the fallen leaves. Eric couldn't tell whether they had stingers or not. Maybe it's already too dark, he thought, but he continued to stare at the picture with his hands behind his head.

"Wouldn't it be just great to live there!" he said out loud. "No more tests about insects because everyone *is* an insect. You just play around in the grass and suddenly the day is over. You can stay up as late as you want with no one to tell you it's bedtime. And when you're tired, take a nap in all those red poppies, or rest in the snail shell, if there's room. In the morning when you wake up, you wash your hands in a dewdrop and you're ready to go! You saunter around a bit, and check in on the egg laying and the hatching of the larvae because you're the only one who knows anything about how it all should go! Oh, how I'd love it."

Suddenly, a soft burst of laughter broke the stillness of the room. It was as though someone had been thoroughly enjoying himself and couldn't hold it in another second. Eric sat up and stared with surprise into the darkness of the room.

"Is anyone there?" he called.

"Ha! Ha! Ha!" replied someone from the wall across the room.

Eric looked up, utterly amazed. The portrait of Grandfather Pinksterblom, founding father of the Pinksterblom family, the severe old gentleman whose beard covered his face like ivy covered a wall, and who lay buried under an impressive gravestone large enough to cover the entire Pinksterblom family, this model of propriety held his nose between his thumb and forefinger and shook with laughter. As soon as he noticed that Eric was looking at him, however, he quickly put his thumb back in the vest pocket where it had lodged for twenty years and stared solemnly at a spot on the opposite wall.

I must have imagined it, thought Eric. But he kept watching the portrait attentively. His heart beat so hard that it seemed as though the whole bed was bouncing. He remained so for a full minute, but nothing happened.

I know, he thought, I'll turn away from the wall, and when he thinks I'm sleeping, I'll suddenly turn around.

A clever idea indeed! Eric lay down and closed his eyes, but he couldn't pretend for long. With a quick twist, he turned around — and saw Grandfather Pinksterblom rubbing the inner edge of the frame with his index finger. He was so lost in his work that he didn't notice Eric at all. Every once in a while he inspected his finger for dust and then rubbed on further, whistling softly to himself.

"I've caught you!" cried Eric. "You're alive!"

What happened then was very surprising — because nothing happened at all. Eric was certain that Grandfather would jump out of his skin — or out of his frame at the very least — but, except for a shake of the head and a gentle smile, he polished blissfully on. Yet what a smile it was! It was full of promises and pleasure in the knowledge that something was going to happen. Eric himself believed that the great adventure he had so long awaited was finally at hand, and he was completely unafraid. His heart beat quietly now and he continued staring at that miracle in the picture frame.

"Would you like my handkerchief?" he asked.

"Mr. Pinksterblom," corrected the portrait.

Eric was reminded that one must always be polite, even in the strangest circumstances.

"Would you like my handkerchief, Mr. Pinksterblom?"

The portrait shook its head. "Thank you, my boy," it said, "but I have everything I need." And he solemnly drew a handkerchief out from under the frame and loudly blew his nose in it, all the while nodding most pleasantly at the little boy in the gigantic bed.

"You'd never have guessed it, would you?" he spoke at last. "That your old grandfather was still alive! Hm?"

"No," answered Eric. "I certainly wouldn't have. But I was sure that something special would happen this evening."

"Oh, this is far from the half of it," said the portrait, smiling mysteriously. "This is just the beginning. There's lots more to come!"

"I thought as much," said Eric.

"You mustn't tell anyone else," whispered Grandfather Pinksterblom, looking around, "but we're all alive."

"*All?*" asked Eric with surprise.

"The portraits," whispered Grandfather.

Eric was about to answer when a voice from the other side of the room said clearly, "Prenez garde, Jean! Il est trop jeune."

Grandfather Pinksterblom's face immediately took on a submissive expression. Eric sat straight up and stared in the direction from which the voice had come, but it was already too dark on that side of the room to see anything.

"What a strange evening this is turning out to be," he mumbled, still staring into the darkness. "Is anyone there?"

"That's your grandmother," said Grandfather Pinksterblom softly. "As a girl, she studied in France."

"Is she the old lady who's sitting in a chair?" asked Eric, who knew all the portraits in the room by heart.

Grandfather brought a finger from somewhere outside the frame quickly to his mouth. "Shhh, boy! Never say that any woman is old, and especially not your grandmother. It could cause a lot of trouble. She's portrayed from top to toe."

8

Eric wondered what that had to do with anything.

"You see," continued Grandfather Pinksterblom, guessing Eric's thoughts, "I and your Uncle Henry, who hangs there across from me, are only painted to the waist. We can't go anywhere. But your grandmother's got her feet and can leave if she wants. She posed for a full portrait. That's the difference."

And as though to illustrate Grandfather's words, the soft tapping of two small shoes was suddenly audible on the other side of the room. Oh, how wonderful! thought Eric. What a marvelous evening! He crept to the end of the bed and stared toward the sound in the darkness. "Can I help you, Grandmother?" he asked politely, at the same time looking questioningly at Grandfather Pinksterblom, whose only reply was a solemn shake of the head and a resigned shrug of the shoulders. But what can I do? thought Eric. I can't leave an old lady on her own. She's probably pacing up and down along the frame, not daring to jump down. He waited a bit, and then slid from his bed to the cold floor. It was difficult to move around in the dark, but with help from Grandfather Pinksterblom, who continually called out directions from his frame — "straight ahead" or "a little bit to the left" — Eric finally stood before the little portrait. It was the most beautiful one in the whole room, in the whole house actually, thought Eric. He had studied it so often that he knew every detail: the old gilded frame, the faded yellow background, and, right in the middle, on her delicate chair, the even more delicate gray-haired old lady in a cloud of lace. But now the chair was empty!

Eric was more alarmed than surprised. He searched the floor to see if she was lying someplace crying, but there wasn't a trace of her. He took the portrait from its hook and held it up in the moonlight by the window. She was really gone! Her chair had been overturned and her flowers lay forsaken on the carpet.

"She's a spirited old girl, your grandmother," said Grandfather Pinksterblom from his frame. "She knows what she wants."

"What should I do?" asked Eric, concerned.

"Oh, you needn't worry. Just go back to bed," advised Grandfather. "She always looks before she leaps," he concluded with a chuckle.

What a nice, friendly man, thought Eric, climbing back into bed, and what a special evening this is! But, as Grandfather Pinksterblom had promised, there was still more to come. No sooner had Eric pulled the blankets up under his chin than he saw a tiny gray-haired woman, no bigger than his thumb, walking toward him over his left leg.

"Don't move, my boy," she called from afar, balancing with her umbrella, "or I'll end up on the floor."

Indeed, it was Grandmother Pinksterblom, slogging her way through the blankets. She was as truly mettlesome a little woman as Grandfather had indicated, and surprisingly agile as she made her way over the folds and bulges of the rumpled bedclothes. She stopped right in front of Eric's nose and looked him straight in the eye.

"Hello, Grandson."

"Hello, Grandmother," answered Eric. And he found it so funny that she was so tiny and he so big that he started to laugh.

"Turn your head!" cried Grandmother Pinksterblom, holding onto her hat by its ribbons. "You'll blow me right down. Did you see my ankles?"

"No, Grandmother," answered Eric.

"Well, thank goodness for that," said Grand-

mother, brushing her skirts straight. "I've never wanted to be the cause of a scandal; everyone knows that." This statement was apparently meant for the other portraits, because Eric heard a timid "Yes" from Grandfather Pinksterblom's direction and a somewhat more convincing "Certainly, certainly," which must have come from Uncle Henry.

"This is not real wool," continued the old woman, looking around her at the blankets. "Half cotton and half goodness knows what." She bent over and took a small bit of the offending material between her teeth. "Garbage," she concluded, throwing the small bite away with disgust, "fit only for rags. What's your name?"

Eric found her conversational jumps as sprightly as her dance over the bedspread, and it took a moment before he could bring out "Eric."

"Eric," repeated the little woman, softly tapping him on the nose with her umbrella. "Look here, look here."

"You're tickling me!" warned Eric. "I'm going to sneeze — haaa-chew!" When he looked up, the old lady was still standing, but she had opened her umbrella.

"Politeness is one thing," she said, "but the whole neighborhood is under water. Still, I guess you didn't do it on purpose."

"Oh no, no," cried Eric immediately. His grandmother looked at him intently, as though to satisfy herself that it was true.

"Yes, I believe you," she said at last, and sat down. To further demonstrate her trust, she clapped her umbrella shut and tossed it into one of the ravines of the blanket.

"So," she continued, "that's that. And what do you think of your grandmother?"

"Oh, you're wonderful," said Eric. "I think you're great — only . . ." he hesitated, "you're kind of small."

To his relief, Grandmother took this well. "I agree with you," she said, nodding her head, "but John insisted on a small portrait because it was to hang between the mirror and the wardrobe and that's all there was room for. Furthermore, he said that he found life-sized portraits a bit ostentatious."

"That's not true," cried Grandfather Pinksterblom. "*You* wanted—"

"Quiet!" shouted a deep voice. "Is this starting *again*? Can't we ever have any peace and quiet around here?"

"Who's that?" whispered Eric, staring into the dark room.

"That's *my* grandfather," Grandmother whispered back, somewhat deflated. "Do you know him?"

"The one on the medallion?"

"Yes, the one on the medallion."

"Oh, he's terrific!" cried Eric. "He's got a wig on and—"

"Shh!" interrupted Grandmother quickly, bringing her index finger to her lips. "Don't ever say that!"

"But it *is* a wig," whispered Eric. The gray-haired lady stared at him for a minute and then smiled.

"You still have a lot to learn, my boy," she said, "but you've also got plenty of time. When you yourself are a portrait, you'll see things differently."

"I don't really understand," said Eric. "Can all the portraits here speak? Are they all alive?"

"Every one," answered Grandmother.

"I still don't understand," continued Eric. "If they can speak, why don't they do it during the day?"

"Oh," answered Grandmother, "they've done that their whole lives and it's nice now not to have to. If your parents knew that we could talk, they'd set us all up in a row in the living room and we'd have to participate in all those conversations! And we've had more than enough of *that!*" All the portraits sighed.

"Yes, I can understand that," agreed Eric, who had often enough been on display in the living room. "I won't tell anyone. But how do you live? Don't you get hungry?"

"Oh, no," laughed Grandmother, "we don't need to eat. We're all flat. Just look." And as she turned full circle, Eric saw to his surprise that she was barely as thick as cardboard, and when her back was toward him, he could clearly read:

A. J. MULDER
Photography and Enlarging
(reduction for groups)

"We've scratched out the price," said Grandmother, speaking into the room, as her back was still facing Eric. "I found it a bit much to leave it there for everyone to see."

Eric lay still, breathing gently. This is the miracle, he kept thinking, the great surprise that I've been expecting for so long. It's here. He looked again at the little lady before him, her wizened face surrounded by her lace cap and her two tiny eyes sparkling like diamonds.

"Everything is alive, my boy," she said. "One just has to see it. Just look at that painting there, with the sheep in the meadow—"

"The painting of Industrious Valley!" cried Eric.

"Yes, the painting of Industrious Valley," repeated Grandmother, without a bit of surprise. "Now, have a good look there."

Eric sat straight up in bed and looked intently at his beloved painting. And there! The sheep lifted their heads, the shepherd waved to him and the white clouds drifted through the blue sky from one edge of the frame to the other!

"Dearest Grandmother," cried Eric, folding his hands in supplication, "let me go to Industrious Valley! I have always wanted to be there, among the butterflies and the bees."

"One has to become very small to do that," said Grandmother. She sounded quite far away. Eric noticed, too, that his pillow had taken on enormous proportions and lay before him like a snow-covered mountain. But he wasn't afraid. He understood that he was growing small—incredibly small—in order to enter Industrious Valley, and he stepped bravely through the folds of his blankets to the foot of his bed.

And now for a standing jump, just like we do in gymnastics, he thought. He clenched his teeth, closed his eyes, and leapt! In a great arching jump, he flew over the edge of the frame and fell into the soft, green grass.

CHAPTER TWO

The first thing that young Eric did in Industrious Valley was cry. Indeed, it is somewhat embarrassing to relate. But didn't we perhaps do the same when we first found ourselves in the painting in which we have now so long been living? It seems to be part of the process, and one must resign oneself to it. And young Eric had one consolation which was not accorded to us at the time: he had wished it upon himself. And that makes a big difference.

"Come on," he said to himself, standing up and looking around. "Let's go and see where the shepherd is."

But the shepherd was nowhere in sight and there wasn't a trace of the sheep to be found. The only things that Eric recognized were the white clouds which floated slowly by in the blue sky, and the green grass that softly fluttered and rustled around him. You can just imagine his consternation as the clouds floated higher and higher until at last even they were invisible to him, and the grass around him steadily grew in height until it towered over him like a gigantic forest.

"Good heavens," mumbled Eric, looking around open-mouthed. "I am still getting smaller. If this continues, there will be nothing left of me at all, and then how will I get home?"

But fortunately, it didn't go too far; things came to a standstill and Eric realized with relief that he would not become any smaller. But, oh, how tiny he had already become! Only when he walked to the edge of the leaf on which he was standing and stared below did he fully realize it. A terrible abyss gaped at his feet, and in the depths he saw the most amazing monsters crawling around, with quivering antennae and clacking jaws. Among them was one particular beast, with a great shiny eye on his back, who stopped suddenly in his tracks and looked sideways up at Eric with that eye, as though to say, "Shall I eat him now, or save him for later?"

Eric quickly pulled his head back and turned around. But still another surprise was awaiting him: right in front of Eric stood a gigantic wasp, staring unblinkingly at him. Being a polite little boy, Eric bowed deeply and said, "Hello, Mr. Waps."

"Wasp," said the wasp.

"Waps," said Eric, blushing. He had always had problems with that word!

"Wasp," said the wasp, without getting the least bit

excited. "It is wasp." He was silent for a full minute, and then said calmly, "Wasp. Wasp. Wasp."

"Waps," said Eric.

The wasp pondered for a moment whether or not to pursue the matter further. Then he shrugged his wings and continued staring motionlessly at Eric in a most disconcerting manner, with two big eyes that stood out from his forehead like tremendous headlights. After a time, he opened his mouth, and shortly thereafter, he asked, "Do you have permission?"

"Permission for what, sir?" asked Eric respectfully.

"Don't you know," asked the wasp, "that you are treading on forbidden territory?"

"I beg your pardon, Mr. Waps, but I—"

"Wasp," said the wasp.

"But I thought that this was a public thorough-fare."

"No," said the wasp, "this is private property. But I excuse you. You are new here, I see."

"Yes, I come from far off," said Eric. He remembered a verse from a schoolbook:

I come from afar
from the land of the sun.

And then he said once more, "I come from far, far away."

"So you couldn't possibly know," observed the

wasp, "that this entire leaf is mine, handed down from father to son — a family estate, you might say."

"Ancestral ground," said Eric.

"Precisely, precisely," said the wasp. "It is ancestral ground. You have hit the nail on the head. I come from a very old family. Allow me to introduce myself: I am van Thinwing." He took a few steps backwards to see what impression this name made on Eric.

"The old branch," he added after a bit. Eric realized that something was expected of him. He mumbled a few words and stared at his bare feet.

"The new branch," continued Mr. van Thinwing, "carries the name van Thinwing to be sure, and they are even related to us, but through a misalliance with the Thickwings, they are somewhat, somewhat . . ." He was silent for a moment and looked off into the distance with a pained expression. "But surely," he concluded, "you know the story."

"Of course," said Eric, perplexed. "I'm terribly sorry for you."

But Mr. van Thinwing already seemed a bit more cheerful.

"Oh," he said, "it is worse for them. May I ask your name?"

"Eric," said Eric with a bow. "My name is Eric."

"Eric," repeated Mr. van Thinwing, wrinkling his forehead. "The name is not known to me. Is that all — just plain Eric?"

"Oh, no, that's only the first part," explained Eric.

"If you say the whole thing all together, it's Eric Pinksterblom."

"Oh, that is entirely different," agreed Mr. van Thinwing. "Old branch?"

"Oh, yes," said Eric. "My father's name was Pinksterblom, and his father, too. *That* was a fine portrait!"

"Oh, really?" smiled Mr. van Thinwing. "The old boys really knew how to live. But they remained gentlemen. That is the difference. It is a pleasure to meet you. And would you care to lunch with us?"

"Gladly," said Eric, who was beginning to work up quite an appetite. "It's very nice of you."

"Then climb up on my back," said Mr. van Thinwing. "I see that you have no wings and it's far too far to walk. I live a ways out of the neighborhood, you see."

Eric climbed quickly up on the bristly back and held on firmly to the yellow hairs.

"Ready?" called Mr. van Thinwing, turning his left eye back to look inquiringly at Eric. Then he immediately spread his noble wings and shot off high into the blue sky.

Oh, how marvelous it was! The warm wind sang in Eric's ears and he practically shouted with pleasure.

"Look at me, Grandma!" he crowed, turning around and waving.

"To whom are you speaking?" asked his host in surprise.

"Oh, sometimes I just talk to myself," answered

23

Eric. "Something suddenly came to me."

"Yes, that happens," said the wasp.

Far, far below, Eric saw the tops of the green blades of grass bend and straighten. Between them, countless tiny animals went about their business, apparently just as big as when he lay in the grass at home and followed their comings and goings.

"Are you comfortable?" asked the wasp.

"Couldn't be better," cried Eric. "And it's so fabulously fast! Can you go even faster?"

"Preferably not," said the wasp. "One arrives so sweaty at the dinner table. And furthermore, my heart's a bit weak."

"Oh, goodness!" said Eric.

"Don't worry, it's not serious, and it's just between us. Even my wife doesn't know. You'll meet her soon. She is also a van Thinwing." Eric noticed that during this revelation, one eye had turned around and was staring at him.

"I see," he said respectfully. "The old branch?"

"The old branch," confirmed the wasp, "although

an impoverished family. But what is money compared with blood?"

"Nothing," declared Eric.

"So right," nodded the wasp. "So right, it is nothing. Although there are naturally problems when one has none at all. I have seven daughters."

"Goodness!" murmured Eric.

"Seven marriageable daughters," continued the wasp. "But I must say, they bring a name with them."

Eric noticed that the eye was again directed inquiringly at him.

"Do *you* have money?"

"Oh, yes," answered Eric, thinking of the three silver dollars in his piggy bank. "A considerable amount!"

The wasp stared at him a while and then turned his eye forwards again. Eric noticed that he hummed and flew a bit faster.

"Here we are," he said at last, coming slowly down. "Do you see that red chrysanthemum? That's home!"

Slowly and gently, they landed on one of the outermost petals, which stuck out, forming a small balcony. "Allow me to lead the way," said the wasp as they went inside. Mr. van Thinwing set his stinger in the umbrella stand and hung his wings on the coat rack. Somewhat anxiously, Eric followed his host. They passed through a long hall where it smelled so sweet that the scent made Eric feel a bit drunk and he had to lean against the pink walls to keep his balance.

"Don't you feel well?" asked the wasp with concern.

"It will pass," said Eric. And indeed he stood up again firmly on his feet.

"You probably also have a weak heart," said the wasp, pleased. "It's a sign of nobility. Will you wait in here for a moment, please?" He opened one of the pink doors and stepped back with a bow, indicating the little square room.

"Excuse me," said Mr. van Thinwing, sticking his head around the corner of the door after Eric had entered. "What was your name again, please?"

"Eric Pinksterblom," said Eric.

"Eric Pinksterblom," repeated the wasp, tasting, as it were, the words in his mouth. "Thank you." And he disappeared.

Eric sat down to wait. It was a charming room. The tablecloth and the upholstery were cut from pink petals, and felt so silky that Eric stood up and let his index finger glide over the smooth surface. The other furniture in the room was also of the utmost delicacy of form, some cut from white lily petals, others shaped from pure beeswax. It all smelled deliciously fresh and natural, so pure and unspoiled that it made Eric thoroughly happy. The walls were made of thin rose petals, so abundant rosy light filled the room. The soft, even glow bathed everything in sight and gave the room an air of infinite fragility, as though one had only to sigh for it all to crumble. Eric remained standing motionless in the center of the room, with his hands tightly clasped together, scarcely drawing breath—he was that afraid he might damage something.

"Would you care to follow me, Mr. Pinksterblom?" asked the wasp, entering through another small door. "My wife is looking forward to meeting you."

Mrs. van Thinwing rose from her chair at their approach. She inclined her head when Eric was introduced. "We are always delighted to entertain a *gentleman*," she said, in a tone that could be taken as a warning. Eric bowed and everyone sat down.

"A gentleman is a gentleman," elucidated Mrs. van Thinwing. "Either one is, or one isn't."

"Precisely right," muttered her husband in confirmation.

Eric felt the atmosphere closing in. It had never occurred to him, watching the wasps flying over the manure piles at home, that they could be so stuffy.

"If one *is*," continued the lady, "then one *is*, but if one *isn't*, well then, one just *isn't*."

"And never becomes one, either," added her husband.

"And never becomes one," reiterated madam, "no matter how hard one tries. And if one is, one doesn't have to try, because one is."

"And so one remains," said the wasp.

"And so one remains," confirmed his wife, "no

27

matter what one does and no matter what happens. Of *that,* we are convinced. I hope you see things in the same light?"

"Oh, yes," said Eric, after a pause.

"That is what I needed to know," explained Mrs. van Thinwing, relaxing noticeably. "Do you take sugar or milk with your tea?"

Tea was served and the conversation became more general. Eric realized that a certain accord had been reached between himself and the van Thinwings, and he dared now to look around a bit. They were seated in a spacious room, where the light fell purplishly through walls which were decorated at regular intervals with small plaques bearing maxims, just as in the hallway of Eric's home. These, however, were of a somewhat more mysterious nature, such as: "One is, or one isn't" and "One who is, is" — sayings whose meanings Eric didn't fully understand, but which nevertheless (or just thereby) filled him with respect.

In addition to the larger area and the still finer furnishings, this room differed from the previous one in that it had a number of tiny windows. The shutters stood open and, to his delight, Eric glimpsed the blue sky and the soft white clouds passing by. The green blades of grass waved gently back and forth, and snails and beetles crawled past, some so big that they temporarily darkened an entire window.

"The thoroughfare is filled with passers-by," said Mrs. van Thinwing, following his gaze, "but there

aren't many with whom one would wish to form an acquaintance."

"Rabble," clarified her husband.

"But there are surely pleasant ones among them,"
offered Eric, noticing a butterfly. "Such pretty colors
—"

"And that is just what betrays them," interrupted
madam. "True aristocracy never parades around in
such a get-up. They know that what counts is in the
breeding, not in the clothing. When one has the proper
breeding, the rest is trivial."

"But when one doesn't have it," added Mr. van
Thinwing warningly, "then one just doesn't have it."

Eric thought to himself that the conversation to this
point was not entirely free of a certain monotony. He
felt an alarming inclination to yawn, and he actually
might have, if Mrs. van Thinwing had not suddenly

turned to him and asked, "To which animal family do you belong?"

Eric stiffened momentarily in his chair.

"I am a person," he said finally.

"A person," muttered Mrs. van Thinwing, pondering. "Let's see. No, I've never heard of that."

"But there is surely a shepherd in the picture," mumbled Eric.

"I beg your pardon?"

"Oh, nothing," said Eric, recovering himself. "I had a sudden thought."

"Certainly excusable," opined his host.

"A person, then," repeated the hostess. "Good. That's that. But now this: does a person belong to the nobility?"

"Not all of us," answered Eric, who felt obliged to represent his fellows in as good a light as possible, "but nonetheless, quite a few. Barons, earls, counts, you name it, we've got 'em. Not to mention the noble souls one finds among the common men."

"Of the nobility, then," decided Mrs. van Thinwing, giving him the benefit of the doubt. "That is point one. And now: how many locomotor appendages does a person have?"

"Excuse me, legs," corrected Eric, respectfully.

"What is that? Legs?"

"Actually, legs are locomotor appendages," admitted Eric.

"Then it is all one and the same," said Mrs. van

Thinwing, "because if legs are locomotor appendages, then locomotor appendages are legs. So: how many locomotor appendages do they have?"

"Usually two," answered Eric, "unless they've been in the war, and then they have only one."

"Have only one," echoed someone in the distance. Eric looked around and in the furthest corner of the room saw a fly scribbling like mad in a small notebook. Eric straightened his pajamas and stood up in order to introduce himself.

"Not necessary, not necessary," whispered Mrs. van Thinwing furiously, waving him back into his seat. "A servant."

Eric sat back down and looked with surprise at the corner.

"He is a sort of secretary," Mrs. van Thinwing informed Eric, still whispering, as though she was embarrassed to say it. "A good boy, but . . ." She made a gesture of dismissal with her hand and stared at the ground.

"No breeding," said her husband sadly.

For a moment, all were silent. Eric felt terribly shy and stared straight ahead at the plaques: "One who is, is" and "One is, or one isn't." He began to grasp a bit more of their meaning, although he was not at all sure that he agreed with them.

"Two locomotor appendages, then. Good," repeated madam. "And my next question is this: do they have a stinger?"

She posed this question as though the future of the world, or Eric's future at any rate, depended upon the answer, and when she had spoken, she leaned forward and stared motionlessly at her guest with those great, gleaming eyes.

"A stinger," repeated Eric, swallowing mightily. "Not everyone."

"Not everyone; that is fine," continued the lady. "That is not necessary, and I would not have expected it. The question is: who *does* have a stinger?"

"Who *does* have a stinger?" echoed the secretary.

"Who *does* have a stinger?" echoed Eric. "That would be policemen and members of the cavalry." He thought of furious Old West battles.

"Good. Policemen and members of the cavalry," repeated the wasp, saying the words clearly and with emphasis. "So it is then. The rest is rabble. And now, my question is this: do *you* have a stinger?"

The question was so unexpected that Eric sat a moment open-mouthed, staring at her. Had he been another kind of animal, he would probably have answered, "Of course not! What kind of a silly question is that?" and been shown immediately to the door. But he was a person, and he answered blushingly, "Of course I do."

"And where is it then?" pursued madam, immediately producing a lorgnette from one of her pockets and scrutinizing her guest from head to foot.

"It is folded up inside my pajamas," explained Eric, stammering. "If I carry it loose, then I'm afraid of breaking it or . . . or wrinkling it."

Fortunately, this answer proved satisfactory to his inquisitors. At a wink from the host, the folding doors were opened and everyone stood up and began to walk to the dining room.

CHAPTER THREE

For quite some time during the conversation, Eric had been aware of the tinkling of glassware and silver and of the muffled whispers from the next room, but it was only when he entered that he realized as much of a to-do had been made for him as on that evening back home when Senator Burnside had stayed for dinner. His mother had spent the whole day shopping, cooking, baking, and cleaning. The most exquisite delicacies had appeared on Eric's plate, but what had surprised him most was when his mother leaned over and said, "It's just what I happened to have around the house, you understand, Senator?"

"But mother," Eric had said softly, but still quite audibly, "you've been working the whole day on this!"

There had fallen a terrible silence, and he had had to go to bed early for a whole week. So he paid close attention when Mrs. van Thinwing said to him, "Sorry you have to take potluck, Mr. Pinksterblom. We weren't expecting company."

"No problem, no problem," he assured her.

"Everything very simple," added his host, waving carelessly at the overburdened table.

"Yes, I see," Eric assured them vigorously. "It couldn't be any simpler."

He shook hands briefly with each of the van Thinwings' daughters, who stood around the table. Each one curtsied in turn. "Lovely girls, aren't they?" whispered the proud father who accompanied him.

"Oh, lovely," mumbled Eric.

"Rascal," said the wasp, poking Eric conspiratorially in the ribs. "Rogue." Eric blushed and didn't know which way to look, but no one seemed to notice.

He was given the seat of honor between his hostess and her eldest daughter, directly opposite Sir P. This was the greatest honor which could be bestowed on Eric because Sir P. was one of the richest wasps in the county. He was taciturn by nature, and troubled by a touch of the gout in his hind legs. He had a great dislike for anything modern. No one quite knew what he had done in the past, or what he did now, much less what he might do in the future, and they therefore addressed him simply, but with respect, as Sir P. He was lodging with the van Thinwings at the time and he did nothing other than get up in the morning, shake his head, and return to bed at night. In short, he was a person to be reckoned with, and Eric could not but be aware of this as he watched the great man tie his nap-

kin under his chin without once removing his gaze
from Eric's face.

"Pardon?" he asked when Eric introduced himself.

"Eric," repeated Eric again with a bow, "but some
people call me Ricky."

"Which is it then?" asked Sir P., looking right over
Eric's head at the wall behind him. "Is it Eric, or is it
Ricky, or is it Eric-Ricky, or Ricky-Eric, or is it none of
the above?" And he smiled maliciously at the confusion his little speech occasioned.

"It's Eric Pinksterblom," clarified the host, "of the
nobility."

"A stinger?" asked Sir P., his soup spoon halfway
from plate to mouth.

"A stinger," confirmed the host.

The soup spoon completed the trip to his mouth,
but Sir P. seemed not yet satisfied. Throughout the
whole meal, he regarded Eric out of the corner of his
eye, and now and then shook his head doubtfully. This
was hardly pleasant, but the offerings of the abun-
dantly spread table compensated for a lot. Great
golden-yellow honeycombs like huge waffles were laid
on his plate and they smelled so delicious that it was all
Eric could do to keep himself from clapping for joy.
He did his very best to appear nonchalant like all the
others, but was apparently not as successful as he had
hoped.

Suddenly Sir P. said, "Don't sit there rocking in

your chair, my good man, behave yourself like a wasp!"

Eric felt somewhat deflated, but forgot it soon enough. He shoveled great clumps of honey greedily into his mouth with his spoon, until he could scarcely utter a word. And when the hostess suddenly directed herself to him, he could only shake his head.

"Appalling," mumbled Sir P., "absolutely appalling!" He pricked a minuscule droplet of honey with one of the tines of his fork and then cut it carefully in half, as though to give Eric a lesson in proper eating habits.

The daughters, on the other hand, couldn't have been nicer. From a waspish point of view, they could even be considered intelligent, and they nodded constantly at Eric with shining eyes.

"Watch out," whispered the oldest daughter, secretly pushing a clump of honeycomb into his hand, "they are all out to catch you."

"I'll save this for later," said Eric, putting the honey in his pocket. "Thank you very much."

Even Mr. van Thinwing seemed to relax, and once everyone had a glass of dew under his belt, the atmosphere became so congenial that Eric even dared offer to sing a song. This proposal was enthusiastically received, with the single stipulation from Mrs. van Thinwing that it must remain polite.

"Okay," said Eric, standing. "It's a song I learned at school. I know it all except the very end. It's called 'The Busy Bee.' "

"The *what?*" cried his host, thoroughly shocked.

" 'The Busy Bee,' " replied Eric, oblivious. "Now listen:

Who doesn't know the busy bee,
The oh so busy bee?
He works all day long,
Humming a song,
Making honey for you and for me.

Perhaps someone knows,
Perhaps even thee,
Someone who does
More work than the bee.
But quick, can you tell it to me?

I can't think of one
Whose work is not done
While the bee is still busy—
It makes me quite dizzy—
He's got no time for fun.

"There's a bit more," panted Eric, because he had sung the song with great energy, "but at any rate, you now have an idea of how highly we people esteem the bees." He looked around expectantly awaiting the family's applause, but to his great dismay, he was greeted by a deep silence. Everyone was staring at his plate, except Sir P., who stood up and stalked out of the room.

"Mr. Pinksterblom," said Mrs. van Thinwing, breaking the terrible silence, "I believe that you have meant well, but you have nevertheless grossly insulted us all."

"I'm terribly sorry," Eric stammered.

Another silence followed. This time it was broken by Mr. van Thinwing. "You have sung a song of praise, Mr. Pinksterblom, to that branch of the family to which I had earlier alluded."

"The Thickwings?" cried Eric, horrified.

"The Thickwings," confirmed Mr. van Thinwing. "It is clear from your embarrassment that you were sincere and intended no offense. I therefore consider the incident closed. Will you hand me the pollen, please?"

But Mrs. van Thinwing felt obliged to further enlighten her unsettled guest. She spoke about the bees in the same tone of voice as was used at home when the family discussed poor Uncle Bob, who had gone off on a boat to the Far East to start a cocoa plantation with a young lady of uncertain reputation. Her chief complaint against the members of this branch of the family was that they had sunk to such a state that they all lived together in a single house. "It must absolutely *stink* there," she said. "It *does* stink there! One of my husband's nephews who works at the consulate and often has to go there on official business (and she laid great emphasis on the word "official") once described it to me. It was *horrible!*" She shuddered, but continued. "Horrible! There's no describing it adequately. Everyone living on top of each other — it makes a decent wasp sick to think of it. And to what end? For honey. But I ask you, Mr. Pinksterblom, what is honey? Honey is nothing. It's breeding that counts. If one has breeding, one has everything."

"But if one doesn't, then one just doesn't," added her husband, slicing a ball of beeswax into small pieces.

"And one never gets it, either," said madam. "Now, Mr. Pinksterblom, the fact that one gathers honey just to have it, just to store up as much as possible, is bad enough. But our family was prepared to overlook that — after all, everyone must decide for himself what he wants to collect —"

41

"I, for example, collect——" began Mr. van Thinwing.

"Oh, hush," broke in his wife, "and don't interrupt me. Where was I, Mr. Pinksterblom?"

"You were storing up," Eric offered helpfully.

"Oh, yes. As I said: if they want to store it up, that's their business. I don't meddle in that, and I have no intention of meddling in it. But that they store up *on consignment*, Mr. Pinksterblom, is unforgivable."

"On what?" asked Eric.

"On consignment. They work for someone else. We don't know their connections and we don't want to, either. But it's a known fact that the honey they slave a whole summer to gather is taken away in the fall by these connections of theirs. And in return, they get . . ." Mrs. van Thinwing was silent. She couldn't get the words over her lips.

"A sack of sugar," whispered her husband. Everyone blushed and stared at his plate.

"Oh, I'm so terribly sorry," murmured Eric. He felt awfully guilty and was not a little embarrassed by his ignorance.

"Therefore," ended madam, "our branch has decided to break irrevocably with theirs and to withdraw entirely into ourselves. Thus even the slightest reference to this relationship is extremely painful to us— especially when it comes in the form of a song of praise for them. On the other hand, you have a lovely voice. You would do us a great pleasure if you would presently give us another opportunity to hear it. We always have a bit of music after eating, you see. It's so good for the digestion. Do you play anything?"

"Father had a bass fiddle," answered Eric (who had begun to speak in the past tense now when he talked of home), "and I could play a little, if it wasn't too difficult."

"That is a happy coincidence," said Mr. van Thinwing. "We could use a bass player. Will you follow us?"

Arriving in the adjoining salon, Eric saw to his horror that the instruments consisted of huge living horseflies, who lay on their backs on the table, feet in the air, with strings stretched across their bellies.

"Are you all in tune?" asked Mr. van Thinwing, tapping one of the flies with his bow.

"Oh, yes sir," came the reply, "all but myself. I think I've sagged a bit. If you would just give me a stretch?" Mr. van Thinwing tightened the strings a bit and bowed. It sounded perfect.

"Your instrument is there, in the corner," said the wasp to Eric, who turned and saw an enormous horsefly leaning against the wall. And as if this horrifying apparition were not shocking enough, the giant insect even reached out to hand Eric the bow, whispering confidentially to him at the same time, "Would you please bow a bit gently in the beginning, sir? I've been standing here idle for almost half a year and I must get used to it again." With these words, he lay himself calmly down on his back and waited patiently, leaving Eric so shaken that the bow fell from his hands. There were tears in his eyes. "Oh, don't trouble yourself about me, sir," said the fly comfortingly. "Page twenty, at the top."

Eric opened the book on the music stand to the indicated page. With relief he saw "The Swallow," which just happened to be something that he could play.

"Ready?" called Mr. van Thinwing. Each of the daughters sat on a stool in front of her respective horse-fly and looked expectantly at Eric. "Begin!" he cried, and immediately struck the first note himself.

It sounded wonderful! Deep, full, and rich, the

sound filled the room and Eric was instantly caught up in the pleasure of making music. He very quickly forgot the horsefly, rolled up his sleeves and bowed so feverishly that droplets of sweat appeared on his forehead.

"Bravo!" shouted Mr. van Thinwing above the resounding strains, tapping out the beat with his foot. "A bit louder now. Good! And now: fortissimo!" It was fantastic! The daughters bowed as though possessed, and father wasp, forgetting his precious dignity, threw his cummerbund to the floor in order to conduct with even more vigor.

Unfortunately, Eric chanced to cast a glance at his instrument during this passage, and he was shocked by what he saw: a quivering, gray-black gelatinous mass.

"Goodness gracious!" he cried, letting his bow fall.

"Where am I?" panted the fly, as soon as the vibrating stopped.

"Don't you feel well? Can I do anything for you?" asked Eric desperately.

"No, thank you," answered the unfortunate insect without opening his eyes. "I'm afraid it's too late." And with that, he breathed his last.

"Come, come, what's going on there in the corner?" cried Mr. van Thinwing. "Why aren't you playing?"

"I can't anymore," said Eric. "He's dead." Two big tears rolled down his cheeks. Everyone lay down his instrument and approached.

45

"What a shame," said the wasp, arms akimbo. "He was a lovely instrument."

"You are not very lucky, sir," said Sir P., who had entered the room just in time to witness the tragedy. "You are constantly causing disasters."

"I couldn't help it," stammered Eric. "It just happened."

"Quite possible," replied Sir P., "but it is rather strange that you always happen to be involved in these unfortunate incidents, don't you think? Hmm?" He looked around meaningfully. "But then," he concluded, "you are not *my* guest. *I* didn't invite you." And he left the room, his back stiff with indignation. Eric felt it clearly: Sir P. had taken the little bit of respect and admiration that Eric had won with so much difficulty irretrievably away with him.

Eric's parting with the wasps was cool, to say the least. "I'll call a bumblebee to take you to a hotel," said Mr. van Thinwing, staring out the window with raised eyebrows.

Eric shook hands all around and climbed up on the bee. It was his intention to give a short speech in defense of the human race, which he felt he had so unworthily represented. He began, "Honored wapses —"

"Wasps," corrected the wasp.

Eric blushed and continued, "I have done a number of stupid things in your company, but it would be wrong of you to think that all those of my kind did such stupid things, too. I am still a child and — ''

"How old are you then?" asked Mr. van Thinwing.

"Nine years old," said Eric.

"Then you are nine times as old as I am," said the wasp drily.

"Let's go!" cried Eric to the bee. "Giddyup!" And off they flew in a wide circle into the darkening evening.

CHAPTER FOUR

Oh, was that delightful! The fresh evening breeze flew deliciously past Eric's head, and the stars shone like diamonds in the sky. It was somewhat cold; Eric pressed his bare feet into the warm fuzz of the bumblebee's sides and looked down curiously. The flower that he had so recently left sank farther and farther away in the distance until it was only a small red point, scarcely discernible. "When you see it from here," mumbled Eric, half out loud, "you might think how wonderful it must be to live in such a flower. But once you've been inside and seen and heard all that goes on there, you're glad to be on the outside once again."

"You have made a very intelligent observation," said the bee.

"Thank you," answered Eric, blushing — he was not used to being praised by the inhabitants of Industrious Valley. "I say it only in passing."

"That is just what is so commendable," replied the bumblebee. "It's no trick to say something important when one has already been pondering for half a day over it. I'm a bit of a philosopher myself, you see, so I know what I'm talking about."

"Oh, indeed," said Eric. "I see, I see."

"If you would care to reach around behind you," continued the bee, "in my pocket you will find a book that I consult occasionally." He coughed modestly.

Eric felt behind him and found the book. Luckily, the moon was bright, so he was able to read the title by bringing the cover close to his eyes. To his surprise it was one and the same as a book in his father's study: *Logica et Metaphysica* stood out in gold letters on the brown leather.

"Boy, oh boy," mumbled Eric with awe, "I have always wondered what that can possibly mean."

"Well, to be honest, I don't entirely understand it myself," admitted the bee.

"But then why do you read it?" asked Eric, surprised.

The bumblebee was noticeably embarrassed. "Well," he said, "I don't actually *read* it. I just occasionally look at the title. It may sound strange, but as soon as I see those words, I start to think a bit more deeply. I begin to feel more like a rational being, gifted with reason and insight—in short, a bumblebee!"

This ending caught Eric unawares. But of course, he realized, that is how a bumblebee would see it.

"Here we are," said the insect, coming in for a landing in the grass.

Eric stepped down and, with a bow, thanked the bee for the ride. "It was so friendly of you, sir," he said. "Thank you very much."

The bee was once again visibly embarrassed. "Hmmmm," he said. "You don't have to thank me. Shall we settle the account now?"

"Settle the account?" muttered Eric, disconcerted. "Certainly. How much — how much do I owe you?"

"I leave that to your discretion, sir," answered the bee, staring into the distance with raised eyebrows, as though the whole business had nothing to do with him.

And when Eric continued to look at him with confusion, he added, "I am a married man, and a father, sir."

"Yes, of course," muttered Eric, searching his pockets feverishly. He knew all too well that there was nothing to be found in his pajamas that could possibly be of any interest to a married man, or a father, for that matter. But so many strange things had happened since he had entered Industrious Valley that he felt justified in hoping for a small miracle. And sure enough, he came across the bit of honey that the oldest wasp daughter had given him.

"Here you are," said Eric.

The bee quickly grasped the honey droplet in his forelegs and turned completely red with excitement. "But my dear sir," he said, "I cannot change this for you."

"That's not necessary," said Eric. "Keep the change!" The words were scarcely out of Eric's mouth before the bee stashed the honey in his back pocket and flew away in a flash, forgetting his book in his hurry.

I have, of course, paid much too much, thought Eric ruefully, eyeing the fast-disappearing insect. I now have nothing left with which to pay my hotel bill, and I find that quite tiresome. Somewhat distrustfully, he looked around for the hotel.

Now, it is no exaggeration to say that Eric was totally undaunted by the dark, but when he turned to find an eye waving up and down right in front of his face and staring unblinkingly at him, it took all of his control not to burst out in tears.

"Hello, eye," he stammered. "Are you alone, or are you perhaps attached to someone?"

"It belongs to me," called a voice from a considerable distance away. "Do you wish to see a room?"

Eric walked past the eye in the direction of the voice, and after a while, he came to a snail.

"Hello, sir," he said, bowing as usual. "Yes, I am looking for a hotel."

"Good," said the snail, speaking very slowly, "very good. But would you be so kind as to return to your previous position? We can't talk like this — I see nothing."

Eric walked past the eye, which was seeking him with all sorts of contortions, and stood firmly and clearly in front of it.

"Perfect," said the snail, "but before we proceed, don't touch my eye. I'm very sensitive about that."

"Yes, I know," said Eric. "If one gives it the slightest tap, you'll roll up and disappear completely inside your house." The eye withdrew in shock.

"It is even painful for me to hear you talk about it," said the voice in the distance. "I really cannot stand it."

"Okay, but I also have a problem with you waving those two eyes around my head," complained Eric. "I don't know which of the two I should address."

"Take the right, then," suggested the voice, "and I will bring the other one inside. Edward! Come here!" And one eye rolled slowly backwards, while the other remained steadfastly in front of Eric's face. It seemed

as though he were speaking to someone through a tele-
phone.

"Did you want a room for tonight?" asked the
voice.

"Oh, yes," said Eric, who was beginning to get cold
from standing so long in his bare feet.

"A room with breakfast?"

"I'd prefer a room with a bed," replied Eric. "I've
actually just finished a hearty meal."

The round eye became oval, as happens when one
laughs, and Eric indeed heard someone laughing in the
distance.

"You are still very young, I see," said the voice in a
soothing tone, "so I will give you a room with breakfast. Further, I can determine from your speech and
clothing (here the eye swooped lower and researched
the buttons on his pajamas) that you are of good family. I will therefore give you running water and—"

"Yes, but it mustn't all be too expensive," called
Eric, who had occasionally gone shopping with his
mother, "or I will have to find another hotel."

"The price will surely be no consideration for *you?*"
asked the snail, looking at him with surprise. This was
just what the men in the stores often said, and his
mother usually said nothing in reply.

"Good," said Eric. "I will take the room." He followed meekly after the snail, doing his best to walk as
slowly as possible.

But, goodness, it was *slow!* Every once in a while, Eric had to stop and give the snail a chance to gain a bit of ground, but in the end he couldn't refrain from asking, "Could you possibly go a bit faster, Mr. Snail?"

"I could," answered the snail calmly, "but I won't."

"This is a good way to drive someone crazy," sighed Eric.

"Drive someone crazy?" repeated the snail, stopping to mull over the idea. "Could it?" He swung one of his eyes around to Eric and looked at him for a moment. "It's not driving *me* crazy," he said then, and recommenced his journey.

"I now begin to understand," continued Eric, after a short while, "what one means by 'at a snail's pace.'"

A long silence followed.

"And just what does one mean by it?" asked the snail finally.

"What does one mean by what?" asked Eric, who had long since been thinking of something else.

"You said," explained the snail, "that you were beginning to understand what one meant by 'at a snail's pace,' and I asked, what *is* meant by that?"

"Good grief," mumbled Eric, "what a conversation! It's enough to make one batty."

"Batty?" repeated the snail, again standing still in order to consider the word. "And what is that: batty?"

"I don't know," answered Eric. "I was just talking to myseif." And there followed another long silence.

"Good," said the snail at last, "but I still don't know what you meant."

"By what?" asked Eric.

"You said," explained the snail again, "that you were beginning to understand what one meant by 'at a snail's pace.' And I asked: 'What is meant by that?' Then you said: 'This is enough to make one batty.' And I said: 'What is that: batty?'"

Eric sighed. "I can't keep up with you," he said.

"Do I go too fast?" asked the snail. "Shall I explain it again?"

"No, no," cried Eric. "I'm never going to understand it."

"Well," decided the snail, satisfied, "if you had just said that in the first place, we could have saved ourselves all this trouble. Here we are!"

He stood still in order to give Eric the opportunity to clearly inspect the hotel. The outlines of a gigantic snail shell loomed up out of the darkness by the light of a lantern that hung outside the door. It was absolutely charming. A small beetle, visible in one of the lighted windows, was peeling potatoes, and he nodded a friendly greeting to the new guest. Above the door hung a sign, but it was blank.

"Lovely," said Eric, "but what is the name?"

"Funny you should ask," answered the snail. "We have already devoted ten years' thinking to that problem. The previous owner, one of my brothers, died from the effort."

"Good grief!" cried Eric.

"Well, yes, it was his own fault. He wanted too much at once. But now it is really high time we took the bull by the horns, don't you think?"

Eric agreed wholeheartedly. "If you like, I'll give it some thought," he promised.

"Oh, if only you would!" cried the snail with delight. "Take a week or so. If you will just warn us when you start in with your thinking, then we can take a break for a while."

"Good heavens!" mumbled Eric. "What incredible creatures!" And he immediately entered the hotel.

"Ho, ho," cried the snail, "not so fast, my good sir! You still have to wait for me — you'll never find it on your own!"

Eric obediently fell in behind the snail. The hotel appeared to consist of one long hallway, which spiraled round and round, getting narrower and narrower. On both sides were small, numbered doors, some with nameplates. As he passed by, Eric saw "J. Gnat" and "A. Daddy Longlegs."

"Those are the residents," explained the owner. "They pay by the month. Those with numbers are the transients; they stay only for a night or two, mostly just passing through, but every one a fine fellow!"

"I wonder," thought Eric out loud, looking at the "Daddy Longlegs" nameplate. "It must be a bit of a problem, putting up so many different kinds of folks. This Daddy Longlegs, for example: what does he do

with his legs?" He had often seen this common garden insect in the yard at home and was curious to hear how such an animal spent his nights.

"Quite simple," said the owner. "If the bed is too short, he just opens the window and lets his legs dangle outside. Where there's a will, there's a way. It's no problem at all, no problem at all."

"Yes, I see," said Eric. "And do you live here, too?"

"Not I," answered the snail proudly. "We snails carry our homes on our backs!"

"But then you can never move to a new one," said Eric.

"That is true," admitted the snail, "and every once in a while one does indeed hear of one of his fellows dying of boredom. It's no joke always to sit looking at the same round walls. It is said that the former inhabitant of this hotel was a victim of it. He was a giant snail from the Ice Age, and so much room suddenly became free at his death, that my brother and I decided to turn his house into a hotel. In five years we had everything ready."

"Except a name," remarked Eric.

The snail sighed. "That's what my brother always said — till the day he died. But the rest is all very nicely done, don't you think?"

"Oh, definitely," agreed Eric, approvingly eyeing the neatly painted doors. "Are all the rooms now occupied?"

"If that were only so," answered the owner. "After the sudden frost last week a large number of the guests never came home again. And I'm left sitting with the unpaid bills! But at the moment, we're half-full just the same. There is a centipede; a caterpillar; the daddy longlegs, as you saw; two bees who have lost their way; a few gnats; six houseflies — terrible payers, sir, terrible payers; a horsefly; three beetles; a June bug; a grasshopper, I believe; and, let's see, yes, a slug; a termite; and a cockroach." He named the last two with some hesitation, and added immediately, "Those last two for just one night."

"And do we all sleep in the same room?" asked Eric, alarmed to notice a mountain of shoes lying in front of one of the doors.

"Oh, no, no," the snail assured him, "the centipede lives there. It's a considerable job every morning to polish his shoes, and he pays double on account of it. Your room is next to his. Would you like to go there now?" He handed over the guestbook and Eric signed his name between a beetle and a caterpillar.

The advantage of always wearing one's pajamas is that one doesn't have to undress at bedtime, thought Eric as he climbed into bed. He fell immediately into a deep and dreamless sleep.

CHAPTER FIVE

When Eric woke up the next morning, his room was brightly lit and the sunshine shimmered on the white ceiling as though reflected from a watery surface. He got out of bed and looked out the window. What a beautiful day! Dewdrops, bigger than a man's fist, sparkled so brightly in the rising sun that Eric almost had to close his eyes against the glare. And every time the wind blew through the gigantic blades of grass, the flickering water droplets slid noiselessly to the ground to burst apart in fireworks of color. This caused such panic in the passing crowd that Eric, each time it happened, could not stop himself from laughing—which was very impolite and caused him to blush continuously.

A spider, furiously insulted, set her arms akimbo and shrieked at him, "Is it all that funny, my dear? Do you really find it such a good joke?" And she screamed and hollered until she was so swollen up with rage that she finally had to sit herself down to catch her breath.

Just as she was about to begin again, an especially large dewdrop rolled down like a liquid avalanche and washed her away. Eric was considerably taken aback.

"Let that be a lesson to you, sir," said a June bug, who had witnessed the entire occurrence, "to conduct yourself in the future as an insect." And the bug nodded solemnly as though to indicate that the sermon was over.

Eric quickly washed his face and combed his hair in the little shard of mirror hanging on the wall. Always wearing pajamas indeed makes life simpler, he mused, continuing his thought of the evening before, because one doesn't have to get dressed in the morning, either. I wonder why everyone doesn't wear them all the time? And he decided then and there to take the matter up with his mother as soon as he got home. But will I ever get home? He thought of it with a sudden shock. I've become so terribly small that she'll never discover me in the painting. Shouting won't help either, because my voice scarcely reaches above the grass. The only solution is to find the frame and crawl back over it.

He felt so much better once this decision was made that he strode full of confidence down the long corridor to the dining room. It was easy to find—you could smell it a mile away! Most of the guests appeared to have already gathered around the table. There were: the two bees, the June bug, the three beetles, A. Daddy Longlegs, J. Gnat, the grasshopper, two flies, and several more whom Eric couldn't immediately place. The slug was apparently still making his way to the dining room, and the centipede was busy putting on his shoes and wouldn't appear until 10:30 at the earliest. The caterpillar was also missing.

Everyone stood up when Eric entered. He bowed and said, "May I introduce myself to all of you at once? My name is Eric Pinksterblom."

"Delighted," they all answered, and the grasshopper even made a small spring into the air.

"You have a lovely name," said this peculiar animal. "Pink- goes up, and -blom goes back down." And he jumped again as though to illustrate his words.

"Don't pay any attention to him," said the bee. "He's always been a little touched. My name is Bee."

"It's not necessary for you to introduce yourselves to me," said Eric. "I know you very well from *Solm's Concise Natural History*. You are a June bug. You are a gnat. You, a grasshopper," and without hesitating, he named practically all of them.

"That is certainly most remarkable," said the bee in amazement. "Do you know him too?" he asked, pointing to a separate table.

"Oh, yes," said Eric, "that is a cockroach. He lays his eggs in garbage and prefers to live in damp, dark places." Everyone applauded and the cockroach looked as though he had been caught red-handed at something not very nice.

65

"And me," said the grasshopper, "do you know about me?"

"You are a grasshopper," answered Eric. "You have jointed legs and a segmented body. You eat leaves and belong to the group of insect pests."

"And what is *that* meant to imply?" asked the grasshopper, looking at Eric distrustfully.

"Oh, absolutely nothing," cried Eric, shocked. "That's just what the book says."

"Oh, that's okay, then," said the grasshopper. He sat down and looked around at everyone with satisfaction.

"It is a striking talent," said the surprised June bug, "to know with whom one is speaking before being introduced. Do you also know who I am?"

"You are a June bug," said Eric decidedly.

"And who am I?" asked a mayfly.

Eric stared intensely at the mayfly and then said, "I recognize you, all right, but you were in the small print section, which we weren't required to memorize. One could, if one wanted to, of course. I think Willy Martin would probably know you."

"And who is Willy Martin?"

"He was the smartest boy in our class," said Eric, speaking again in the past tense. "He sat a few seats in front of me. He knew everything, even the small print, but he was never a showoff."

"In any case, you certainly belong to an intelligent class of animals," decided the bee. "If you would like to take a seat next to me, you will surely feel at home."

"Oh, good, thank you," said Eric.

He was surprised that all the insects were suddenly so polite and respectful toward him, until his eyes fell on the book, *Logica et Metaphysica,* which he had left lying there yesterday. With a shock, he realized that the damage had already been done.

"One so seldom meets intellectual animals these days," said the bee, sprinkling a bit of pollen on his bread, "and scholars who have written books are rare as hen's teeth. I happen to have a special respect for Latin books—one feels the weight of every sentence.

But what does it mean? Yes, that is the question: what does it mean?" And he looked around, smiling.

"Oh, it's not all that difficult," mumbled Eric.

"Oh ho!" cried the beetle. "That's just what all you scholars say, and that's exactly how you give yourselves away. You are clever, but you won't fool us!"

"I nose around a bit now and then myself," said the bee. "It's part of my work, actually. Though not wanting to compare myself with you, to be sure, I must admit that I have acquired quite a little knowledge in my time, if I do say so myself."

"And what is it that you do?" asked Eric, who found it tiresome that everyone was so modest, and would gladly set the bee in the limelight for the moment.

The bee blushed with pleasure. "Where have I left it now?" he mumbled, searching diligently in his pockets. "Ah, here it is!" And he handed Eric his card:

E. J. BEE
Sweet Merchant

"Well, yes," said Eric, "but what do you sell?"

"What do you mean?" asked the bee.

"Don't you see?" asked Eric, rereading the card. "It's hardly to the point to describe your personality. Wouldn't it be better just to come right out and say what you are selling?"

"But I *am* a sweet merchant!" cried the bee.

"Still, you should write what you have to sell," insisted Eric.

The conversation immediately became so complicated that it took quite some time before the June bug could straighten it out.

I do everything wrong, thought Eric sadly to himself when all the shouting was finally over. He ate a bit of lettuce and looked shyly around him. But everyone was already busy eating and talking again.

"You see," said the beetle, "that's how it is here. Very friendly. You talk a little, and you eat a little, and before you know it, the day is gone! When I first arrived here, two years ago, I was passing through with a piece of horse manure that I was bringing to the market to sell. Just passing through. It had gotten late, evening had fallen, it was getting cold—you know how those things go."

"Oh, yes," said Eric.

"Let's stay here for the night, I thought. It's a good hotel, conveniently situated, not too expensive—"

"Excuse me, but could I interrupt a moment?" asked Eric quickly. "Exactly how expensive is it?"

"Everyone pays in his own coin," answered the beetle. "I pay three leaf lice per week. But that won't help you, since you're only staying one night." And he sunk away in thought.

"Do you think the owner would be satisfied with the book?" asked Eric, blushing.

The beetle was shocked. "But Mr. Pinksterblom,"

he said, "that is much too much! Two, or at most three pages would be very generous."

Thank goodness, then, that's settled, thought Eric. It was as though a weight had fallen from his shoulders and he could finally look around and calmly observe the company in which he had landed. And what an amazing company it was! On his left sat the daddy longlegs, who hadn't the faintest idea what to do with his arms and legs and was kicking everyone's ankles under the table. On the other side the beetles were again complaining that their arms were too short to reach the serving dishes which stood in the middle of the table, and that the others were meanly taking advantage of the situation to do them out of their just desserts—not to mention the main course! Others kept getting their antennae tangled up with those of their neighbors and Eric was constantly being called

upon to unravel the knots and calm down the entangled parties. The slug (who had arrived in the meantime) had his own problems. He was so slow that every time he finally decided on a particular dish, someone else was there ahead of him. In the end, he withdrew under the table with a mournful grimace.

Everybody's got troubles, thought Eric. People *are* the best off after all. But almost immediately he was proven sadly mistaken. At that very moment, the long tongue of the bee shot out with lightning speed, stealing a droplet of honey practically out of Eric's mouth. Eric could only look around in dumb amazement, hoping to see where it had disappeared to.

"Ha, ha," laughed the bee, sticking out the tip of his tongue. "I'll bet you can't do that, Mr. Pinksterblom!" Everyone laughed wholeheartedly at the joke and Eric finally had to laugh, too.

They all went back to chatting and joking, and the grasshopper, easily over-excited, suddenly began jumping around the room like an out-of-control pogo stick. When the other insects noticed how attentively Eric was observing that beast's antics, they too began to demonstrate their skills. A respectful silence fell as the bee showed how it was possible to hover almost unmoving at a single point in the air. The horsefly showed how he could take his head in his forelegs and set it down a bit in front of him to make bathing more convenient. At that, however, some of the others hid the fly's head and the poor fellow ran hopelessly here and there throughout the room, trying to find it again. Everyone was having such a good time that even the cockroach at the separate table dared a faint grin. Eric himself was about to climb up on his chair and give the small speech which had caused such a sensation at Uncle Frederick's dinner, when the snail appeared in the doorway.

"Gentlemen," he said nervously, "might I interrupt you a moment? I'm afraid something has happened. No one answers in Room 14 — Mr. Caterpillar's room. As you know, I always bring his breakfast leaves to him in bed, but this time he didn't answer. I thought: He's still sleeping. I'll come back in an hour or so. Good. I went back, I knocked, I called — nothing! I'm afraid . . . he's been so quiet and uninterested these last few days . . ."

Everyone rushed off to the room in question. It was an agonizing trip: only the snail knew the way, and at every turn it was necessary to wait until he caught up with the crowd.

"For heaven's sake!" cried the grasshopper, springing against the ceiling with impatience, "can't you go any faster?"

"I'm going at top speed," panted the snail. "Any faster and you can add my corpse to his!"

This observation brought the seriousness of the situation again to the forefront. "It seems to me," said a spider, as they all stood waiting at the next corner, "that our good friend had become more and more re-

clusive in recent days. It was as if a secret sadness was growing inside him. He would sit for hours staring silently into space and if you asked, 'What's troubling you, old boy? Can I help you?' he just shook his head sadly.''

And one by one, each of the others recalled peculiar instances from which it appeared that they had known all along that something was not right. "Maybe it has something to do with a woman,'' suggested a horsefly, and everyone looked very glum. Eric found it secretly flattering that he was allowed to be present during such grown-up conversation.

"Gentlemen," said the snail, when they finally stood before the door, "whatever happens, I ask that you use the greatest discretion and that we try as much as possible to keep the authorities out of this. The good name of the hotel is at stake."

"But the hotel doesn't even have a name — good or otherwise," observed the cockroach, who stood at the back of the crowd. No one replied to this remark and the snail withdrew into his house for a moment to calm himself before continuing.

"I think it would be best if we all shouted 'Caterpillar!' at the same time. I'll count to three. Ready. One . . ."

Everyone waited.

"Good grief!" cried the grasshopper, "have you fallen asleep, or what?"

"No, no," mumbled the snail pensively, "I suddenly lost count."

"Oh, I could scream," said the grasshopper. "Ready, gentlemen? One! Two! Three!"

"Caterpillar!" echoed through the hall — followed by a deep silence.

"We'll have to break down the door," concluded the grasshopper. "Heave to, men!" And he sprang against the door with such force that it seemed to crack. But it remained firmly shut, no matter how hard they pushed and banged.

"It's good solid material," said the snail, not without some pride. "You can see that for yourselves."

"If you would slide one of your eyes through the keyhole," said Eric to the snail, "you could look around inside and see exactly what's going on."

Everyone expressed admiration for this insight. The snail stepped back a bit, carefully placed an eye at the keyhole and began creeping slowly forward. "Don't push, anybody," he kept saying. "The slightest misstep could be fatal."

All held their breath. The eye remained inside the room for a full minute, and no matter what the owner was asked, he remained speechless with surprise. Finally he stepped back. "Gentlemen," he said with a quivering voice, "a crime has been committed. Mr. Caterpillar is sitting completely tied up in a corner of the room."

There was a disconcerted silence, but to Eric, the news rang a bell. "That is a chrysalis," he said.

"A what?" asked the snail.

"A chrysalis, a cocoon," said Eric. "In order to become a butterfly, the caterpillar has to spin himself into a cocoon. And then after a while, he comes out as a butterfly."

"I don't get it," said the dung beetle.

"I don't either, entirely," said Eric, "but it's true. I read it in *Solm's*."

"Okay, okay, but why does it all have to happen in my hotel?" cried the snail. "Couldn't he have found another spot for his carryings-on?"

"Actually not," said Eric. "It happens suddenly and then there's no stopping it. The caterpillar gets sleepy, stops eating, begins nodding his head—"

"What did I tell you?" interrupted the spider. "I knew it all along."

"Begins nodding his head," continued Eric, who knew this section of *Solm's*, small print and all, perfectly by heart, "and withdraws into a dark, preferably still, corner. Larger varieties even bury themselves in the ground. The entire cocoon is spun in a few hours. Then hibernation begins, lasting two to six weeks, depending on—"

"Excuse me," interrupted the snail, "what's that you say? Two to six weeks? And is he going to occupy my best room all that time?"

"It is advisable not to disturb the cocoon in any manner," concluded Eric, repeating the final sentence from *Solm's*, "so you must leave him alone."

"I don't give a rap for *Solm's*," said the snail. "I want my money!"

"You couldn't ask more than half the usual room and board price," said the bee, "because he's not eating anything and doesn't require any services."

77

"It's not actually all that simple, though," said Eric, "because who is really responsible for the bill? The caterpillar has indeed had the use of the room, but he won't be here anymore. And the butterfly will certainly appear, but he hasn't used the room."

"My head is swimming," said the snail. "I'll never understand it." And without taking another step, he withdrew into his house to commiserate with himself.

"This will be his death," said the beetle to Eric, as they wandered back to the dining room. "The question of a name for the hotel has already taken its toll, and this will surely finish him."

Eric said nothing. He was considerably surprised that in the presence of this miraculous occurrence, the only thing that concerned anyone was money.

At the same time, the incident had solidly established his reputation for scholarship with the guests. From all sides, he was bombarded with questions about the laying of eggs, the care of larvae and everything else under the sun. When he happened to remember the right chapter, Eric gave a precise answer, but mostly he just said, "Do exactly as you've always done and everything will turn out fine. And if it's your first time, follow your instincts. You all have instincts, you can rest assured. *Solm's* says so! And if you follow them, you'll be doing exactly what *Solm's* says. If you feel like laying an egg, lay an egg! It will be just the right time. Try not to lay it earlier or later than you feel like it, or things will get all messed up!"

The insects were astounded. "We are doing every-thing just as it says in *Solm's*?" they asked. "Without having read it?"

"Definitely," answered Eric. "Exactly so!"

And that night, as he lay in bed, Eric thought: it is indeed peculiar. They are certainly much smarter than I am. It takes me a whole evening to learn a chapter, and they do precisely what it says, without ever having read it. What a wonderful thing, instinct! I wish I had it. And he fell soundly asleep.

CHAPTER SIX

Eric's early days in The Snail Shell (as it came to be known, following his suggestion) couldn't have been happier. New guests were constantly coming and going and they all wanted to discuss their habits and lifestyles with him. He often found it hard not to laugh — the insects were all so obviously real, yet at the same time they looked so much like mechanical reproductions from horror movies, with their huge clacking claws and constantly searching antennae. Some even had multiple eyes dispersed over their bodies so they could turn their head to blow their nose and continue to regard Eric attentively from somewhere in the middle of their belly.

What surprised Eric the most, though, was the large number of legs on which they transported themselves. It seemed to him that they could easily miss half of them and not notice the difference. (He was, however, prudent enough to hide this opinion from his new acquaintances.) For their part, the insects were equally astonished that Eric was able to manage with only two. "Don't you ever topple over?" they asked. "Doesn't it take a lot of energy to keep yourself standing up?"

"Not in the least," answered Eric, who surprised them further by carelessly raising one leg and unabashedly continuing the conversation while standing on the other. This trick was constantly met by a storm of applause, and Eric found that he couldn't repeat it often enough to satisfy his astounded audience.

His Saturday night bath was also an event of considerable interest. Everyone stood around the bathtub watching as Eric stepped out of his pajamas. That one could remove one's skin whenever and wherever one pleased was remarkable enough, but that one had a second skin underneath, well, they couldn't stop talking about it. "Why don't you just walk around in your second skin?" they asked. "It's much more beautiful, and it fits you so much better. That first one is so baggy and sloppy, while the second fits as though you were poured into it."

"It's not allowed," said Eric. "It's immoral."

"What's that: immoral?" asked the snail.

"Immoral is when you're naked," answered Eric.

"Then, I am immoral?" concluded the snail uncertainly. The other insects also looked perplexed.

"Well, I don't actually understand it all too well myself," said Eric. "I only know that it's immoral for a person, unless you are taking a bath, or have just been born, and then it's okay."

Another curiosity worthy of careful observation was Eric's prayer ritual. All the insects stood staring open-mouthed with surprise. "What are you actually doing now, Mr. Pinksterblom?" asked the snail, who normally acted as spokesperson for the group.

"I'm talking to God," explained Eric.

"And who is God?" asked the snail.

"God is He who made me," said Eric, who was no slouch when it came to the catechism.

"And who made *us?*" asked the snail.

"Jos. Th. Brennan," replied Eric, giving the name that was scrawled in the lower right-hand corner of the painting.

"Then that is our God," concluded the snail.

Eric was appalled by this blasphemy, but there was hardly anything he could say to refute it. I'll explain it again later, he decided. It's okay for a while, but for the long run, it has got to be stopped. And he decided that he must talk with someone about this world that was really only a picture.

But talk with whom? He had plenty of friends; scarcely a day passed that any number of hotel guests didn't ask him to accompany them for a walk. But, to be honest, Eric was not so fond of complying. Some of the insects, like the centipede and the mayfly, walked too quickly, so that all his attention was needed to keep up with them without stumbling. And when they finally returned to The Snail Shell, Eric was always dead tired, and had not exchanged a single word with his companion. Others of the insects, like the snail and the earthworm, walked so terribly slowly, and so often stood completely still, that Eric got dizzy with impatience, and longed for the excursion to be over. The only one who walked at about the same speed as Eric was the cockroach, but Eric found that in his position as "member of the nobility," he could scarcely continue to keep such company without bringing scandal to the family name.

What most convinced him, however, to keep the secret of the painting to himself was the dawning realization that none of the insects had the slightest interest in his life. They all rambled on exclusively about their own — eggs and larvae, hibernation, migration, courtship in the spring, and the scarcity of good ironweed and proper goldenrod. The bee would hold forth for hours on the preparation of pure honey, and how the quality could be spoiled by workers who were only out to further their own interests. He once devoted an entire Wednesday afternoon to the question of the breeding of leaf lice. Eric had all he could do to keep from yawning with boredom. Once the spider cornered Eric and told him everything about the design and building of a proper web, and the best way to lure a fly and bind it up. She related how she had dropped a stitch once the previous spring and her whole web had come out cockeyed. Then she described, down to the smallest detail, the restoration process necessary to return the web to its proper shape. When Eric had made his bow and withdrawn with relief to his own corner, a caterpillar sat down next to him, casually crossed all of his legs as if for a long stay, and began to explain comprehensively the difference in taste between the main-vein and the side-veins of an apple leaf. He further noted that there were actually caterpillars who preferred main-veins to side-veins, which strongly spoke of poor taste and low birth.

And so there was no one to whom Eric dared confide that this whole existence, which they all found so tremendously important, only played itself out within the cheap frame of a second-rate painting that any day might be tossed into the trash if his mother should decide to redecorate. Was it even possible to explain to these self-satisfied inhabitants that the frame itself existed, and that life really only began on the other side?

Eric became quieter and quieter, and withdrew more frequently into his own corner after meals. Sometimes a tear slipped down his cheek. "I guess you're thinking of spinning yourself into a cocoon," said the snail, concerned. Eric only shook his head sadly, giving added ground to the snail's suspicions.

But it is always darkest before the dawn. One morning, just when Eric had made the dangerous decision to leave and search for the frame on his own, the door of the breakfast room opened and a butterfly entered. Everyone put down his knife and fork and stared openly. Even Eric was surprised. He had seen plenty of butterflies at home, but of course never so large and at

such close range. It was an enchanting sight. The transparent, delicately veined wings were a pale lilac and in the middle of each one blazed a purple peacock-feather eye of such opalescence that it seemed to shimmer with a life of its own. There were little folds and wrinkles in the wings, as though they had just lately been unfurled, and the butterfly itself seemed to be so young and tender. She stood precariously on her slender legs and looked around with surprise.

"So!" cried the snail at last, "here's our old caterpillar back with us. Thirteen days and fourteen nights we've waited. Can you pay your bill?"

The butterfly fluttered her wings. "I'm afraid I don't know what you mean," she said shyly. "I woke just now in a tiny room and have come here for information. Could someone tell me where I am?"

"That's the limit!" cried the snail, outraged. " 'Could someone tell me where I am?' For fourteen days that good-for-nothing sat here eating my best cabbage, and then occupied my best room for two weeks further. I won't sit still for it — you're going to pay up, my friend."

"Don't shout so," said Eric, coming quickly to the rescue. "The butterfly can't help it if she was first a caterpillar. According to *Solm's,* it has to be that way."

"I don't give a rap for *Solm's!*" cried the snail. "I want my money."

"You certainly don't have any appreciation for one of the miracles of nature," said Eric, annoyed, "but you can have your money! Here!'' And he tore the entire first chapter from *Logica et Metaphysica* and threw it scornfully on the table.

"That's better," said the snail, snatching it up. "I apologize."

The butterfly approached Eric and gently dipped her antennae. "I don't really know what's going on," she said, "but I believe I owe you my thanks."

"Oh, no," said Eric. "There are still so many chapters left and I am happy to have been able to help you. I am also glad that everything worked out so well: you were in your cocoon precisely the correct number of days."

"In my cocoon?" asked the butterfly shyly.

Eric explained to the best of his ability what had happened. "Indeed, mademoiselle," added the mayfly, licking his lips, "you would not be standing here as you are now had not Mr. Pinksterblom insisted that we must leave you alone."

The butterfly turned her great sparkling eyes to Eric and looked unflinchingly at him. "Why have you done all this for me?" she asked, tremblingly.

But Eric didn't answer. He looked into the big eyes, which reminded him of the eyes of the deer in the zoo back home. He seemed to see the same desire for the open fields and the forests. He felt that before him was an *animal* different from all the many-legged *insects* surrounding him who asked nothing and wanted nothing but to scratch around in the earth and lay eggs in shallow holes, who could only, as far as he knew, talk about themselves and their own limited interests. And suddenly he felt very happy, as though he had found a true fellow. "You don't have to thank me," he said. "You have made me much happier than I have made you."

The butterfly ate and drank very little at breakfast. She sat quietly on her chair in the middle of all the chatter and stared shyly in front of her. Her great violet wings were spread out on either side of her chair like two bodyguards. Eric could not stop thinking how much she looked like a beautiful angel. Every so often, he saw her lift her quiet gaze and look longingly out the window, where white clouds drifted lazily through the blue sky, and he thought to himself, I see it now! She's just like me! Just like me!

That very evening he revealed his secret to her. The butterfly listened attentively and pondered a while when he was through. Then she said, "You saved my life when I was ugly and defenseless. Now that I have wings, I want to help you. You must climb on my back when I fly off to the sun and the flowers. Alone, on foot, you'll never make it." And they agreed to depart early the following morning.

Eric couldn't sleep a wink that night. He lay wide awake, staring at the great white moon through his window and listening to the soft noises of the endless night. How miraculous it all is! he thought. The gentle night breeze blew through his hair as he leaned out the window.

"You are restless, sir," said a glowworm, passing by on his rounds. "I've seen many a youth staring out his window at the stars. Seeing you like this, it wouldn't surprise me in the least to hear that you also write poetry. If I may give you some advice, don't be bothered, sir. It all comes to nothing, and the world is no better for it. Be happy with what you have. That's my slogan. Weekdays your cabbage leaf, and Sundays a delicious leaf louse — what more could one want?"

"I want to get out of here," said Eric. "I want to fly high in the air. I'm leaving tomorrow, on a butterfly."

"There it is!" cried the glowworm. "I've come too late, I see. You are a poet, sir, a dreamer. And you will never come to a good end. A distant cousin of mine was like you. One day he spun himself into a cocoon and when he reappeared he wanted nothing to do with any of us. It ended very badly."

"What happened?" asked Eric.

"He flew away and we haven't heard a word from him since."

"Then why do you say it ended badly?"

"I see," said the glowworm, "that you are one and the same type. You don't understand that it's hardly proper to go flying about. Keep your feet on the ground, sir. That is safe and proper. But you must decide for yourself. I wager you'll have occasion to remember my words. I bid you good night, sir." The glowworm turned off his lamp and was lost in the darkness.

Still, Eric remained determined. When the butterfly tapped on his window a few hours later to see if he was ready, he scrambled over the sill without hesitation, all washed and combed for traveling. He left *Logica et Metaphysica* behind on the night table.

"It's going to be delightful flying weather," said the butterfly, looking around appreciatively. "Little wind and a cloudless sky."

Eric clapped his hands. "Let's be off!" he cried excitedly.

"I don't really know if I can fly," whispered the butterfly anxiously. "I've never done it, you know. But something in me tells me that I can."

"That's instinct," said Eric. "Don't give it a thought, just go to it!" And the butterfly fluttered her wings and rose straight into the sky. "That's perfect!" cried Eric, who had climbed up on an ironweed leaf to observe the test-flight. "Now to the right! Beautiful! Terrific! Now come in for a landing." And the butterfly alighted right at his feet. "It was wonderful," said Eric. "You are a natural flyer. Shall we go?"

"Just tell me the direction," said the butterfly. "You came from there, so you must know where it is."

"If it were but true," said Eric. "*We* have only intellect, which is not as helpful as instinct in a case like this. Let's go as high as we can, and see what we can see."

"Okay," said the butterfly. "Here we go!"

And the earth sunk away beneath them. The butterfly didn't fly quite as smoothly as the wasp or the bee. To be honest, it was a choppy flight, and Eric had to hold on for dear life to keep from tumbling off.

"How's it going?" the butterfly called, not looking around.

"Terrific!" said Eric, staring ahead in terror.

"You mustn't hold on so tightly," said the butterfly. "It's still all so new!" And shortly thereafter she panted, "I can't go any higher. Do you see anything?"

Eric looked around and gave a small cry of pleasure. The earth stretched out below as far as he could see, the grass sprinkled with diamonds, twinkling in the sun. But as hard as he looked, Eric could see no sign of the frame. "I don't see anything. But I really don't mind anymore. Just fly where you will. Everything is so beautiful!" So on they flew, into the rising sun.

CHAPTER SEVEN

So began a carefree, joyous time for Eric. Together he and the butterfly let themselves float on the warm air, descending every so often into a flower-filled meadow, almost drunk with the rich smell of so many blossoms. Neither of them had much experience of the world yet, so everything was a surprise and a delight to them. Whenever they chanced to meet a beetle or a bug who had landed before them, they stammered their apologies and stumbled clumsily away as though in search of something until they could again ascend toward the blue sky.

Eric loved honey. At home he was only allowed to have it on Sundays, and even then in only a very limited quantity. Now he could eat as much as he pleased, and when a rare flower's supply was particularly delicious, he filled his pockets to capacity, or tied a great golden glob in his handkerchief and secured it around his neck. (As everyone knows, there is a great difference between honey from a rose and a jasmine and a clover. The connoisseur recognizes the difference instantly.) The butterfly would procure the honey with her long tongue and set it, neatly rolled into a ball, on a leaf for Eric; he himself had nothing to do but climb up and feast to his heart's content. By the third day, the first of the buttons burst from his pajamas.

"You eat too much," said a beetle, who happened to be present when the unfortunate incident occurred. "If you keep on like that, you'll explode one of these days. Just see if you don't!"

"Oh, come now," said Eric, who was really a little embarrassed.

" 'Oh, come now' nothing," said the beetle. "I speak from bitter experience. I had a brother who had a sweet tooth like yours. One day we heard a huge bang and when we all ran to see what had happened, all we could find was one hind leg and an antenna."

Eric immediately dropped his clump of honey and resolved to eat less in the future. He also began to do gymnastics, using the long, overhanging blades of grass as parallel bars.

One morning, while they were sitting on the edge of a dandelion taking a breather, the butterfly suddenly began to tremble all over.

"What is it?" asked Eric, alarmed. "Are you sick?" The butterfly did not answer immediately.

"There!" she cried suddenly. "There she is again!" A large butterfly circled a peony, landed for a second, and then descended further into the long grass. She was somewhat more delicate of build than Eric's companion, but of the same coloring and pattern.

"I must follow and see where she lives," cried the butterfly. "What a beauty!" He was gone in a flash.

"It's a *he!*" muttered Eric, who was familiar enough with similar events in the lives of his older brothers to know what was going on. "I had been thinking it was a *she.*" Eric felt vaguely disappointed and sat waiting for the butterfly's return with his knees drawn up under his chin.

He hadn't long to wait. Suddenly the butterfly returned and cried urgently, "Quick! Quick! Climb up on my back. I know where she lives!"

When they arrived, the lady butterfly was just disappearing into a poppy. "Remember now," said Eric, counting the flowers, "third from the left and second from the front. What a lovely house! Shouldn't there be a nameplate somewhere?"

They walked completely around the flower but couldn't find anything with a name on it. "Family and titles don't matter anyway," said the butterfly, who was still trembling all over. "Did you see her face, her figure, her deportment? An angel!"

"I didn't see anything," answered Eric honestly. "It all happened so fast."

They climbed up on an unoccupied dandelion nearby, in order to keep the neighborhood under surveillance. It was almost evening when the lady butterfly suddenly appeared again between the petals and flew off for a breath of fresh air. They flew quietly after her, keeping their distance.

"You must catch up with her and start a conversation," advised Eric. "This will get you no place."

"Yes, I guess you're right," said the butterfly, shaking considerably. "But what can I say to her?"

"I don't know," said Eric. Then, thinking of his sisters, he said, "Tell her how pretty she is; I think they all like that. A little present is also always good."

"She's above all *that*," said the butterfly. "That's just the problem; *she* wouldn't be taken in by that sort of thing."

"Possibly," said Eric, "but, nothing ventured, nothing gained. That's what my brother always says."

"Your brother . . ." began the butterfly, but then he only smiled sadly and shook his head.

Back home, they sat up late talking.

"It's something entirely new," concluded the butterfly, "something much purer than anyone else has ever experienced. I stand completely alone. Oh, I believe I shall never be able to eat another bite."

"My brothers always said the same thing," replied Eric, "but they managed to put away quite a bit just the same."

The butterfly shook his head and silently wandered off through the flowers. Eric watched as the shadow of the delicate form passed before him against the darkening sky and he felt himself very much moved. It's not true, what they say at home about butterflies being frivolous, he thought to himself, and I shall tell them so if I ever get back again.

The moon was now high in the sky, pouring her silver light over the plants and flowers. It was a quiet night, with an occasional breeze that gently rustled the high grass. Eric sat in his favorite position, with his knees pulled up under his chin, and stared above. The vastness and beauty of the silent skies made him feel happy and peaceful. It's strange, he thought. I'm sitting here inside a poppy watching a love-sick butterfly, and I don't feel one bit out of place.

The following morning when they awoke, the butterfly announced his decision.

"I don't dare approach her," he said, "and giving a present is just too ordinary. All that remains is poetry. We must send her a verse."

"But that is also a present," said Eric.

"But it's poetry," said the butterfly. "Poetry is always appropriate."

They began at once. The butterfly found a clean new lily leaf and Eric cut a sharp point on a pine needle. The poem itself, however, presented numerous difficulties, and although it was nearly lunchtime before they had finished the first verse, they found it still a bit too much on the somber side:

> *This thought I can't bear anymore —*
> *My head is constantly spinning;*
> *My heart is mournful and sore —*
> *That you I haven't been winning.*

"It is indeed profound," said the butterfly, reading it once more, "but I'd like to give it a more practical tone." And they continued:

> *It's easy for you to ignore me,*
> *And leisurely gather your honey.*
> *But it's not long before*
> *Cold weather is in store*
> *And then, where will you be without me?*

"That'll make her stop and think," said the butterfly.

"Maybe so, but it's not very friendly," found Eric.

"As long as the end is passionate," said the butterfly. "It's the end that counts."

Come then to me and let's marry.
There isn't a reason to tarry.
We'll share all our joys and our sorrows
And have so many happy tomorrows.

"Very good," said the butterfly when Eric read the whole thing through. "Very tastefully done!"

The letter was folded up and entrusted to an ant for delivery. They spent a restless night. The butterfly sighed constantly and Eric could hardly sleep a wink. The next morning, it appeared that their concern had been justified: the lady butterfly did not appear. Nor was she visible the following day. The butterfly was fading away right before Eric's eyes.

"Earlier," he complained, "when I was still a caterpillar, I spent all day creeping over a cabbage leaf, without a care in the world. I was certainly ugly, but I was happy. Life went calmly on. I knew no women, and hadn't the slightest thought about poetry. Then came that restlessness and the desire for a better life. I spun myself into a cocoon and woke up with a head full of dreams and a pair of brightly colored wings. But the peace is gone — that's what you get for having ambition!"

Eric thought of the glowworm and was silent. Somewhere in his heart, the idea grew that nothing worthwhile comes easily. The residents of The Snail Shell married and laid their eggs in the same blissful contentedness with which they patiently chewed away on their daily cabbage leaves. This was something different — more delicate and lovely, but painful as well.

"It'll all work out," he comforted the butterfly. "My brother walked up and down one girl's street every evening for three months before anything happened. It always seems to take forever. Only Uncle Bob wasted no time at all, and everyone was angry with him."

And everything did, indeed, work out in the end. When almost all hope had been given up, the ant brought a letter from Papa Butterfly in which they were invited for some "serious discussion followed by an intimate dinner." And it couldn't have gone better.

The "serious discussion" was of the briefest possible duration; the anxious parent only wanted to be assured that the prospective groom was a hard worker. He didn't want to be too demanding, but he felt that three clumps of honey per day was the minimum basis for the establishment of a proper household. He smiled his satisfaction when the butterfly assured him that there were even days in which he had collected five to seven honey droplets. As proof, Eric showed where he was missing a button from his earlier days of gluttony.

Love, said Papa Butterfly, was all very nice, and he felt the greatest sympathy for it, but in the end, what really mattered was honey. Honey provided a foundation and solid support—all the rest was just decoration. He had also been in love in his time (and here he smiled) and he still thought back with pleasure to those bygone days (the smile grew broader). But when the little caterpillars started coming, he had burned his poems and become a serious insect. Still, he didn't wish to discourage anyone. "On the contrary," he insisted. "A talent for poetry is very handy for the long fall evenings. And your second verse shows foresight, an eye for the practical, and a businesslike approach to things."

Eric sat quietly and listened. He would never have suspected that butterflies could be so practical and it surprised him and saddened him somewhat that it was the second verse that had made such a good impression. "I found that part particularly unsympathetic," he said.

The butterfly father turned his gaze to Eric and let it rest there for a minute. "You are still very young, Mr. Pinksterblom," he said. "You do not yet realize the value of honey. But you will. One learns by experience. You must first have a full summer behind you."

"I have *nine* full summers behind me," answered Eric stubbornly.

"That just makes it worse," said the butterfly father. "You may be one of those unfortunate beings who completely lack a sense of responsibility. But there is still hope. Wait till the first caterpillars arrive, then you'll talk differently."

The "intimate dinner" was much more pleasant. Besides Mrs. Butterfly, there were twelve butterfly children, each more lovely than the last. The slightest movement and their wings rustled like silk dresses. At the foot of the table, the youngest children, who were still caterpillars, sat eating everything in sight and saying nothing. The table was so full with many different, delightful dishes that Eric was at a loss for words to describe his happiness. At home, it had always been necessary to first work his way through so many tiresome things — soup, meat, vegetables, salad — that he didn't have enough hunger left to do justice to the dessert when it finally arrived. But here, *everything* was dessert, one thing sweeter than the last, and all in such an array of charming colors and shapes.

"It's just what we happened to have on hand," said Mrs. Butterfly, noticing his surprise.

"Of course," said Eric quickly. "I understand completely." He stuck his fork into a lilac honey clump and soon had his mouth so full that for the next few minutes he was completely unable to join the conversation.

"You just have to take what comes," said Father Butterfly. "We always eat whatever's easiest." He frowned threateningly at one of the smaller caterpillars who seemed ready to say something, then took up his knife and fork and busied himself with eating in such a manner that all the children silently followed his example.

It was a true party. Eric's butterfly friend cheerfully related all their adventures together and devoted much time and praise to the way that Eric had stood up for him in The Snail Shell, saving him from certain death. For this, Eric received a kiss from Mrs. Butterfly, and

Father Butterfly proposed a toast to his health. "Many thanks, Mr. Pinksterblom," he said. "If you hadn't done that, I'd still be sitting here with twelve unmarried daughters. Now one at least is on her way!" On his side, Eric couldn't have been happier as he watched his friend beaming at his new bride and shyly blowing her kisses.

An unexpected surprise came when suddenly, halfway through the meal, a tiny caterpillar crept over the edge of a basket of eggs that had been standing in the corner. He looked with surprise at his new surroundings and was greeted by all with a cheer.

"It's because it's so warm in here with so many of us," explained the mother, taking the baby in her lap and smiling proudly. "I hadn't expected this one until tomorrow, the little rascal!"

Father Butterfly said how happy he was, but insisted nevertheless that the egg basket be placed in the hall. Times were hard enough, he said.

Everything goes so naturally in the animal world, thought Eric to himself, remembering the birth of his younger brother. No messing with diapers and bottles. You just lay an egg, and everything else takes care of itself. Why, the cute little dickens isn't even a minute old and already he's worked his way through an entire cabbage leaf!

The butterfly father stood up then and tapped his dew glass. He wanted to say a few words — which somehow ended up being a bit more than that, but no matter. The path of marriage doesn't only wind through the cabbage patch, but also through the briars. Still, that shouldn't discourage anyone worth his honey. It's precisely in those times that one shows his mettle. Then one sees if the marriage is based on honey or not. Because only a marriage based on honey will survive. Sooner or later, all others will perish.

Honey was the be-all and the end-all. Honey, if he might be permitted to so express it, was the meaning of life. He didn't want to force his opinions on anyone. He spoke merely as an insect of experience. In other times, as he had earlier hinted, he had felt differently about things. He could still remember as though it were yesterday the moonlit night when he and his wife had first gone for a walk together and had talked for hours about the wonder of the flowers and the stars. He had even read a poem to her, if he remembered correctly. Indeed, he admitted, he had been in love. He did not understand why one should not acknowledge one's weaknesses, so long as one always remembered that in the end everything turns on honey, and on honey alone. Because all too soon, the young caterpillars start arriving. As Mr. Pinksterblom had just informed him, according to the expert Mr. Solm, it was only a question of three weeks, and there you were already. He would say nothing further; he was an uneducated man, and his wife had always managed without Mr. Solm. He only wanted to emphasize this: that things will happen, and happen quickly.

And finally, as concerns a dowry, he was terribly sorry to have to announce that due to necessary economizing, there wouldn't be one. The times were difficult, if not precarious, and he was glad to be able to fill the twelve mouths of his family. A scant few moments ago the thirteenth, whom he welcomed heartily, had arrived, and a basket full of eggs just waiting to hatch stood in the hall. All were most welcome, that was not the point. But a dowry was out of the question. His wedding gift must be his daughter, and he felt this to be more than adequate. She was a lovely child, with beautiful wings, delicate antennae, and a quiet modesty. So saying, he declared the new couple to be married and wished them all the best.

Everyone was moved. Mrs. Butterfly dried her eyes with a rose petal and said that she agreed with everything her husband had said.

That's taking the easy way out, thought Eric to himself. I believe I can do better. And he stood up and tapped on his glass.

"A toast from Mr. Pinksterblom!" cried the excited new father-in-law.

"Honored butterflies and capitillars—"

"Caterpillars," corrected a voice.

Here I go again, thought Eric, but he continued bravely. "I, too, am so happy that all has turned out as well as it has, and that we are sitting here so happily together at this wedding feast, even if it is only 'potluck.' Because we all know how easy it might have been for things to go wrong at the last minute. So often something comes up to spoil everything. My brother Theo was very much in love with a girl, but her father was against it; and when he found another, her father was all for it, but his own was against it; and then he found still another, and both fathers were in favor, but the girl herself was not—and so it goes."

"Your brother has been very busy," observed the father butterfly.

"Indeed," continued Eric, "he always had something going. I often saw him sitting in his pajamas writing letters by the moonlight that came through the window. And he wrote endless poems."

"But no honey," interrupted the butterfly father, shaking his head.

"Finally everything worked out for the best," said Eric, "and now I am an uncle. It was the same story with my brother Peter, and Jack is still at it, and no one believes that he will ever succeed. I only want to show that it is often very difficult to get the lady of one's choice. How very happy my friend must be that he has found her and that no one is against it!"

Everyone applauded, and then it was time for the newlyweds to be on their way. Eric climbed up on a poppy leaf to see them off. He waved and waved, until his neck was stiff and he could see nothing more than dancing spots before his eyes. Then he looked about him and sighed deeply.

He was alone.

CHAPTER EIGHT

To truly understand how Eric felt as he struggled through a seemingly endless clump of grass, one would have to be nine years old, dressed in pajamas, and trying to cross a huge, overgrown forest. He had already been walking for three days and was beginning to get discouraged. Sometimes he was so dizzy with hunger that he had to sit down and rest against a blade of grass before he could go on. When threatened, he defended himself weakly with a pine needle.

One cannot live on edible mushrooms alone, and most of the flowers were far too high for Eric to reach. He tried climbing them, but even though he had cut quite a figure on the jungle gym in the schoolyard back home, he could now get only halfway up before sliding back down the slippery stems to the ground. He could reach the smaller flowers with less difficulty, but there's not much honey to be found in a buttercup. It is not only inferior in quality, but so scant in quantity that it hardly justifies the dangerous climb. And we must admit, even honey gets boring after a while. One spoonful is delicious, and even a cupful is manageable if one eats steadfastly and constantly reminds oneself that it would be a treat at home. But there are limits! When one has nothing to eat but honey, day in and day out, one begins to detect, as strange as it may sound, the first signs of dislike. And finally, one longs so for a plain old potato or a slice of dry brown toast that just the thought of these simple edibles is enough to make one's mouth water.

But there was no one to feed these to Eric. From all directions, he saw nothing but suspicious glances and unfriendly looks, and he was grievously saddened to note that public opinion had so decidedly turned against him since his departure from The Snail Shell. Could it be because I left everything behind? he wondered every once in a while, and because I am now poor? But I mustn't let myself think like that. However, it did indeed appear to be the case; the boldness with which the insects accosted him increased perceptibly as he grew hungrier and shabbier. Now and then one would even plant itself directly in front of him, clack its jaws and stare attentively, as though contemplating how such a tender young morsel would taste. At such times, Eric needed all his determination not to turn tail and run for it. But he knew that flight would mean certain death. Any of the insects could easily overtake him in a very short distance. So he would take a firm stand with his pine needle spear steadied against his foot, aim the point at the threatening insect's hairy chest, and say slowly and clearly, "Another step, my friend, and you're off to the Happy Hunting Ground!" This sentence actually came out of one of his brother's Westerns, but it was very effective nevertheless. Usually the invader would take a step or two backward, think carefully for a minute, and then satisfy its hunger with a passing leaf louse.

When this was not the case, Eric would gently begin to hiss. He would squint his eyes and crouch down like a cat, ready to spring. This was his own invention, and it usually worked wonders. But if even this didn't do the trick, he resorted at last to attack. Such a desperate measure had only been necessary twice so far. The first time, the enemy was a horsefly. The beast had suddenly appeared from behind a large pebble and advanced unhesitatingly with ever-lengthening strides. Eric's jab with his pine needle was so well placed that the fly's left eye popped right out of his head and rolled away like a marble. The owner stood dumbstruck for a moment, looked Eric up and down with his remaining eye, and walked off shaking his head.

The second time nearly cost Eric his life. It occurred when he tried to walk through a particularly thick clump of grass. He would ordinarily have walked around it — one never knows what dangers lurk there — but this time, tired and hungry, he decided to try the shortest route. Holding his spear ahead of him, he forced his way through the undergrowth. Suddenly, the point of his pine needle got stuck on something. Eric looked up to see a glistening thread stretched tightly across the narrow path. As though bewitched, he stood there staring. All the colors of the rainbow were reflected in that delicate filament, and Eric thought at once: there must be people here, little people like me, because only people could spin such an exquisitely beautiful fiber.

Joy and thankfulness welled up in him. He ran quickly forward to inspect the thread more closely. It was spun from an unusual material that Eric had never seen before: smooth and shiny, without any irregularity whatsoever. It was stretched tightly across the path, and even when the wind blew, it didn't move. It seemed to be attached to something else that kept it in balance. But no matter how carefully Eric looked, he couldn't discover what this might be. On one side, the thread disappeared diagonally, high into the air; on the other side, it was anchored to a small clump of earth.

Eric had become very cautious after all of his adventures. He walked back and forth along the thread before he dared to touch it. Then, slowly, he reached his hand out, barely brushing the thread with his index finger. But that was enough — he was stuck! In his frantic efforts to free himself, he grabbed the thread first with his whole hand, and then also with his other hand. It was *terrible!* The filament glued itself to his fingers like flypaper, and no matter how hard he pulled, there was no escaping.

Had Eric been simply an insect, he would most likely have gotten his entire body wrapped up in the thread in his fear and panic and have been truly lost. But he was no insect; he was a person. So he stepped back as far as he could to think. Then he placed his feet next to his hands on the thread, sat down, clenched his teeth, and stretched back with all his might. Slowly, the thread stretched, too — thinner and thinner, until, at last, it snapped! Eric rolled backward over the ground, and at the same time, very nearby, he heard a peculiar rustling, as though a delicate construction that had been supported by the thread had collapsed. A suspicion hit him like lightning; he jumped up and whirled around, spear in hand, and not a moment too soon. Right in front of him stood a tremendous spider, shaking with fury on her crooked, hairy legs. The point of the pine needle was aimed right at her throat.

"Don't move, madam," warned Eric, who remembered to be polite even in such terrifying circum-

stances. The spider stood motionless and looked Eric up and down with sparkling eyes.

"You naughty boy!" she screeched in a shrill voice. "Why have you destroyed my web? Why, why, why?" She stamped in fury. "I've been working on it for three full days, and now you come along and ruin everything!"

In her rage, she had swollen up to twice her original size, and her seven eyes rolled around in her head like shiny marbles.

"Calm down, madam, calm down!" cried Eric, shaking from head to toe. "I'll pay off all the damage with my savings."

"Your savings!" shrieked the spider, who was absolutely beside herself. "What good are your savings to me? What possible use can I have for your miserable savings, you wretched creature? Are you trying to make fun of a poor old widow?"

"Well, I could help you fix it," offered Eric desperately. "I can tie loops and bows and hold the thread. You'll be surprised how fast it will go. We'll throw in a few slip knots, and a few grannies, and before you know it, it will be done!"

"Oh really?" yelled the spider. "Just like that! All done! Well, well, Mr. Know-It-All. Ha, ha! But who, may I ask, will provide the material? It's just a question, you understand, just a simple question. Who, my dear — *who?*"

"Well, umm, you'd have to do that yourself, of course," muttered Eric. "I would, if I could, but I don't have any."

" 'I don't have any,' " mimicked the spider sarcastically, getting more and more excited. "And do you think that I'm made of the stuff? That I can just churn it out like butter? Without any raw material, you stupid — "

Here she interrupted her own lecture and looked thoughtfully at Eric. "Come a bit closer, little one," she said, speaking suddenly with a voice dripping honey, "and do lower that nasty pine needle! I'm not going to hurt you. Come, come!" Eric was silent and kept his pine needle resolutely at the ready. "Oh, come now, my boy!" lisped the spider, rocking soothingly back and forth on her long legs. "I was just fooling around there a moment ago. I do that every once in a while; I scream and I holler, but I'm just exercising my lungs. Moving the air around a bit. Clearing out the cobwebs, so to speak! Ha, ha! And then I can sit peacefully again for hours. You understand. You're surely not angry, my little morsel . . ." She swallowed gluttonously and fluttered her eyelashes at Eric.

"Oh, certainly not," replied Eric quickly, although he was feeling more uncomfortable with every passing minute.

"Pretty little boy!" lisped the spider, trying so hard to look friendly that her eyes all crossed each other. "Come a bit closer so that we can discuss the necessary

repairs. Let's see . . ." She closed a few of her eyes for a moment to indicate her conciliatory frame of mind.

"No, thanks," said Eric decidedly. "We can talk just as well at a distance. I've watched spiders like you often enough at home and I know exactly what you're planning. Besides, at school I gave my best test answer on spiders. I know all about you. You can't fool me!"

The spider squinted a number of her eyes in answer and crouched down on her legs. It was an almost imperceptible movement, but Eric recognized it immediately. Quick as a wink, just as the spider leaped at him, he raised his spear on high. He watched as the point sank deep into her chest and she slowly slid down the needle toward him like a giant black bead. He felt something warm and sticky dripping around him; and then, everything went dark.

When Eric opened his eyes, it was the following day and the sun was already high in the sky. He looked around and sat up in surprise. A group of serious-looking beetles, dressed in black jackets with coattails, stood in a circle around him. As he sat up, they all shook their heads regretfully. The oldest leaned over and said, "We were just trying to decide whether you were dead or not. Pity, pity!"

"What is a pity?" asked Eric. "I am, as you see, not dead."

"No, we see that," mumbled the insect, looking Eric over searchingly, "and I suppose you haven't the

slightest inclination to lie down on your back with your legs in the air?"

"Definitely not!" said Eric indignantly.

"Well, we can wait," said the insect. "Do as you please!"

"Wait a minute!" said Eric. "I don't understand. Where is the spider?"

"The spider is already buried," answered the black insect. "If you'll stand up, you'll see the grave right next to you." Eric did as suggested and stared into the hole. There lay the spider, staring back at him. She was dead as a doornail, but one of her legs continued to move slowly back and forth.

"Reflexes," explained the beetle, noticing Eric's shocked expression. "Sometimes it lasts for hours. I once buried a grasshopper leg and when I dug it up the next day, it was still twitching. One gets used to the strangest things in this business." He smiled at the memory, but became immediately serious again. "It'll be over shortly and then we can cover her up. While we were waiting we dug a hole for you, too."

"For me?" squeaked Eric with alarm.

"If you'll look to your left?" suggested the beetle. And not two steps away, Eric indeed saw a long, shallow hole, exactly the shape of his own body.

"We were just about to lay you in it," continued the insect, "when you sat up. So it was all for nothing. I was actually against it from the beginning. I thought that all was not quite in order with you. You definitely

looked suspicious to me. When one has already been in the business for three years, one recognizes the signs."

"Been in *what* business for three years?" asked Eric.

"Grave-digging," answered the insect, bowing deeply. "And all these gravediggers are also gravediggers." They all bowed and looked at Eric.

"I'm sorry," he said blushing, "that I can't be of service to you." No one said a word, but they all kept watching Eric expectantly.

"Gentlemen," he said at last, "if you want something, please say so!"

"We have but one wish," said the first gravedigger, who seemed to sympathize with Eric, "and that is that you should die. Then we can get on with our work."

"But I am not about to die!" cried Eric.

"Ho, ho!" said the gravedigger, smiling. "Don't say that so fast. Things can always take a turn for the better. How often have we not seen someone come to for a while, yes, even walk around a bit, and then lie down forever. Yes, it can still all turn out for the best. I always say: 'Where there's life, there's hope!' "

"But you're turning it around," said Eric, dismayed. "I know that saying, too, and it means that one can always get better again, no matter how serious the situation seems."

"An interesting interpretation," said the gravedigger, considering, "but I believe that you are mistaken. The real meaning is that anyone, as long as he is alive,

could die at any minute, and that one must therefore never despair. But for now, I believe we are wasting our time waiting for you! Come on, fellows, let's finish up here!"

All the gravediggers turned around and, with their back legs, they kicked dirt into the spider's grave. They all joined hands to stamp the earth down flat, accompanying their strange dance with the following song:

> *Pound, pound, pound!*
> *Here's one in the ground!*
> *The one who's dead*
> *Is the other's bread*
> *And so the world goes 'round!*

"What a clever song!" said Eric, "And it goes so well with the stamping feet."

"Oh, it's not over yet," said the gravedigger. "Listen."

> *Beat, beat, beat!*
> *The ground down with your feet!*
> *Soon this treasure*
> *In full measure*
> *Will give us a tasty treat!*

"When are you going to dig her up?" asked Eric, as they all wandered off together.

"That takes some time," said the gravedigger. "Every so often one of us comes back to see how it's going. If she's ready, he'll give a whistle through his fingers and we'll all come running to dig."

At that moment, a long, high-pitched whistle sounded in the distance. The gravedigger immediately took off like the wind, with the others close behind. "If you'd care to join us," he called over his shoulder, "then come along, but you'd better hurry!"

Eric ran as fast as he could, but his two legs were no match for the six of all the others. When he arrived panting at the place where everyone was gathered, they were all already seated in a large circle with mouths full, and they looked suspiciously at him.

"What was it?" asked Eric, as soon as he had caught his breath.

"A horsefly," said the gravedigger, chewing mightily. "Just enough to go around."

"But couldn't you have saved a small piece for me?" asked Eric. "I feel so dizzy . . ."

"Business is business," said the gravedigger. "You should have run faster." He swallowed the mouthful that he had been chewing on and looked with mixed emotion at the hind leg that he still held in his hand. "One must never shortchange anyone," he said finally, "and if I were to give this to you, I would be short-changing myself." He stuck the leg in his mouth and swallowed it in one gulp.

He seemed, however, to be more sympathetic now that he had a full stomach. "If you'd care to come over to my house for a bite," he said, "I'm sure that my wife would have no objections. Nothing fancy, of course."

"Oh, thank you," said Eric. It was really high time that he received such an invitation. He followed his host with difficulty over a molehill and crept after him into a narrow passage.

CHAPTER NINE

"It gets wider very soon," said the gravedigger, pushing against the ceiling with his horny back. "If you start right off with a wide entrance, then everyone and his brother feels free to wander in and out. Look, here we can already walk next to each other." And so they proceeded along the widening passage with its gentle downward slope. At irregular intervals, small patches of sun coming through holes in the ceiling lighted the ground. The passage floor was strewn with discarded legs, wings, antennae and leftover worm segments.

"What do you think of the place?" asked the gravedigger.

"Well, to be honest, it kind of stinks here," answered Eric. "And why doesn't anyone clean up this mess?"

"What mess?" asked the gravedigger, looking around in surprise.

"All those legs," said Eric. "It's disgusting. Some of them are still twitching. It really needs to be cleaned up."

The gravedigger shook his head silently. "You certainly have strange ideas," he said finally. "All this is a sign of prosperity. Look at that piece of worm, for example. The front and back ends are missing, but the middle still darts around here and there as though to say: 'Try me! I'm delicious! I'll melt like butter in your mouth!' But what's wrong? Don't you feel well?" Eric had sat down right in the center of the hallway.

"Don't you feel well?" repeated the gravedigger, excitedly circling around him. "Would you like to lie down with your legs in the air? That's the best thing. I thought everything would turn out all right. You just lie down and I'll go dig a hole, okay?" And he immediately began kicking up the dirt with his hind legs.

"Don't bother," said Eric, standing up. "I feel better already."

"Really?" asked the little black insect. "Are you sure? Come and see what a nice hole this is." And he lay down in it himself with his legs high in the air and his eyes closed peacefully.

"No, thank you," said Eric. "I won't be needing it."

"Okay," said the gravedigger without the least trace of anger as he scrabbled right-side up again. "Then we'll just have to wait a while. Death has no favorites and sooner or later we all have to stick our legs in the air. But here we are!"

He stepped aside to let Eric enter a large, gruesomely decorated room. The entire floor was covered with bones and skulls, and a collection of bodies of every imaginable sort of beetle stared out at the visitor from where they had been leaned up against the wall. The ceiling was low, and here and there a bit of spooky light penetrated through tiny holes, barely illuminating the room. The only living things in the entire macabre scene were the little gravedigger children, who sat everywhere on the ground, playing with the bones and skulls, and now and then uttering cries of delight.

"Thoughts of death," said the father, watching his offspring at play, "have great educational value. And through this sort of play, they learn the shape of all the different animals, so that they will later be able to make the holes exactly the right size, saving them unnecessary digging."

"Who do you have with you, Albert?" asked a voice from the darkness.

"Indeed, what is your name?" asked the gravedigger. "My wife would like to meet you."

"Oh, excuse me," said Eric, immediately stepping back and taking a bow. "My name is Eric — Eric Pinksterblom." His words echoed in the large room. Mrs. Gravedigger stared at him in surprise.

"But Albert!" she cried out. "This beast is still alive. He's moving!"

"Yes, dear," said the gravedigger. "He didn't want to."

"And why not, sir?" asked the missis, directing her gaze at Eric.

"Didn't want what?" asked Eric. "I'll be glad to, if

you'll just tell me what!"

"He's moving again," cried the lady. "What's going on here, Albert?"

"As you said, dear, he's alive." The gravedigger sighed unhappily.

"Well then, there's nothing to be done," decided the missis. "We'll just have to wait. In the meantime, Mr. Pinksterblom, you are most welcome here. Please make yourself at home."

They all sat down around a clump of earth and Eric listened with interest to the gravedigger's report of his trip. It was an amazing story for human ears. The insect had encountered a number of pitiful horseflies, but they were so skinny that they weren't worth the trouble of burying. He had also dug up a June bug in an advanced state of decay and it had tasted delicious. There were rumors, continued the gravedigger, that there was a dead earthworm lying beside the dam, but the smell wasn't yet strong enough to confirm this with certainty. He promised himself—

"May I interrupt?" Eric broke in suddenly. "What do you mean by 'the dam'?"

"The dam," explained Mrs. Gravedigger, "is the end of the world."

"And where is the dam?" asked Eric, breathless with excitement. "Please tell me!"

"I believe our guest is feeling unwell again," said the gravedigger, watching Eric with anticipation. "Am

I right, Mr. Pinksterblom?"

"Oh, I'll be perfectly fine," pleaded Eric, "if you'll just answer my question."

"Then I certainly won't," said the gravedigger. "I'd be a fool to work against my own interests."

But at this moment, Mrs. Gravedigger showed that women everywhere share the same humane qualities: she felt sorry for Eric. "As soon as you've had a bite to eat," she said, "and you feel a little stronger, climb up on the highest blade of grass that you can find. In the distance, you'll see what we call the dam — a high, smooth wall made of wood. No one knows what lies beyond."

"Oh, but *I* do!" cried Eric, beaming with joy. For there, after all, was his own land, the land of people. And somewhere there, the Pinksterblom family was sitting sadly around their table, mourning their little Eric, who had disappeared one day and couldn't be found. Oh, how he longed to hear his mother's voice again!

"What are you thinking of trying?" asked the gravedigger, pacing nervously back and forth. "I don't like surprises. What have you got up your sleeve?"

"I want to climb over the dam," said Eric. "I don't belong here."

The gravedigger shook his head. "What kind of nonsense is this?" he asked. "I don't understand it, and I doubt if it's a good idea. Stay where you are and be

content with what you have. That is my advice. Earn your bread, lay your eggs on time, and let the sun do the rest.''

"All well and good for you," said Eric, "but that has nothing to do with me. I belong on the other side!"

"Just snobbishness," said the little gravedigger. "If I and the others can stand it here, so can you. I know those ideas of yours. Two of my ex-wife's sons also talked like that: 'There must be more than this!' they said. 'We don't belong here!' I put a stop to that immediately, before it was too late, and now they each have a thriving undertaking business. In three months, when we're both a bit older and wiser, Mr. Pinksterblom, we can discuss this again. But now, let's eat! There's a real treat waiting for us, something extra special!" The little insect stuck his nose in the air and sniffed at the aroma that drifted in from the room next door. Even Eric's mouth watered. It smells just like lamb chops, he thought to himself, but, of course, it's not.

He followed the gravedigger, who led him, half dancing with pleasure, into the other room. The little gravediggers stopped their playing and followed their parents and Eric. "You see," said the host, sniffing the delicious odors, "these are the things of *this* side, Mr. Pinksterblom! Grab hold of them and enjoy them! What do you know of the other side? Nothing!"

Everyone sat down at the table and looked at the large, steaming horsefly that lay on a platter in the center. "A lovely beast," said the gravedigger, sharpening his knife and casting an expert's glance at the offering. "A bit thin in the ribs, but a beautiful, fat stomach. What would you like, Mr. Pinksterblom, a wing or a thigh?"

"May I just ask," said Eric, swallowing heavily, "is that a horsefly?"

"Indeed it is," said the gravedigger, "and one of the choicest specimens I've ever dug up. I can well imagine your surprise, Mr. Pinksterblom. It is indeed a beauty!" He expertly sliced off a piece and laid it on Eric's plate.

Hunger is the best cook, they say, and it was no less

true for Eric than for anybody else. Although he indeed started in with a quivering fork, he was soon eating with as much appetite as his table-mates, and by the end of the meal, he had to admit that horsefly made a delicious dinner.

"The best is yet to come!" cried the host, wiping his forefeet as he looked with expectancy toward the kitchen door. "But I won't tell you what it is. It's a surprise — a small surprise in honor of our guest!" He bowed and Eric bowed back, and everyone felt just wonderful.

"Undertaking," continued the insect, "is without a doubt the best profession that there is. One learns to know all kinds of animals, large and small, and the special merits of each one."

"That is true," said Eric. "You put that very well."

"Yes, didn't I?" exclaimed the gravedigger. "Each one has its own flavor and texture and surprises. With one it's the back that's the tastiest, and with another, the belly. Would you care for some more?"

"No, thank you," said Eric, pushing his plate away, and feeling suddenly a bit queasy.

"They all talk big," continued the gravedigger, smiling, "but sooner or later, they all end up on my table. That is their destiny. All those scrabbling creatures think that they are living, but that's looking at things from the wrong end. They are simply on their way to the grave. That is the true picture. It takes longer for some than for others, but in the end, they will all wind up in the same place. I periodically go out and look around to see how things are progressing."

"That is a very pessimistic view of things," said Eric, wrinkling his forehead.

"The truth always sounds pessimistic," said the gravedigger, "but if you think it over for a minute, you will have to agree — the whole world is there for the gravediggers!"

"Whatever do you mean?" cried Eric angrily. "That's not true at all! Who do you think you are, anyway?"

"But it *is* true," replied the gravedigger, smiling. "Take, for example, this horsefly who lies here before us, Mr. Pinksterblom. She devoted her whole life to becoming big and fat. After a long struggle, she finally made it. I won't go into all the problems that she had to overcome to achieve her goal. She managed to succeed. But for whose benefit, Mr. Pinksterblom? Who profits from all that effort? Me! It was all for me! Perhaps you will say: 'but it was also for me.' "

"No, I wouldn't say that," said Eric.

"And why would I disagree with you?" continued the gravedigger as though he had never heard Eric's interruption. "Because it is, after all, in *my* interest that you also eat well. I find it delightful that you are getting fatter, and I'll even help you do it, as you see. I could just burst out singing sometimes when I go up above ground and see how everyone is sweating and working to earn their daily bread, how every effort is made to become round and fat. Look at this! I think to myself. Isn't this terrific! Sometimes when I see a spider sitting in her web, or a beetle scuttling past me, I think: he's doing just fine — just a bit more flesh on the ribs and he'll be all set! You can't imagine how comforting it is when one understands the purpose of everything. I don't even mind when they occasionally eat each other up; it may make a difference in the quantity, but it is always compensated for in the quality!''

Just then, something awful happened! It all went so fast that later Eric could never remember exactly how it actually happened. From far in the distance, they suddenly heard a fast-approaching rustling sound, and someone shouted, "A mole! A mole!" Eric saw the gravedigger and his wife go pale with fright and stare at each other with terrified expressions. Then the little insect took a tremendous leap over the table and tried to reach a small niche in the wall on the other side. His wife grabbed two of the little ones by the arm, and all three tried to hide in a small hole. Eric, without thinking what he did, let himself fall flat on the ground with his arms stretched out over his head. He was just in time. He felt the soft mole fur glide over his back like a caress. When he looked up a moment later, the room was as bare as a vacant house. Even the bodies on the wall and the remains of the horsefly on the table had vanished. A huge hole had been broken into one of the walls, and when Eric turned around, he saw an even larger hole on the opposite wall. It opened into a wide passage from which he heard someone loudly smacking his lips as he disappeared in the distance.

"How terrible!" mumbled Eric, sitting down for a minute. "This is really awful!" He looked around in astonishment at the now spotlessly clean floor, and suddenly the words of the gravedigger came to him: "Death has no favorites, and sooner or later we all have to stick our legs in the air."

CHAPTER TEN

We shall now hear of Eric's adventures as he attempted to find his way above ground. It was nowhere near as simple as one might have thought. All of the underground passages looked surprisingly alike, and after wandering for a long time, it was not unusual to find oneself in exactly the same spot where one began.

Eric did meet several animals from whom he might have asked the way, but most of them were in too much of a hurry to listen to him. The few who stood still long enough to listen cast such covetous looks at his arms and legs that Eric himself preferred to rush off and take his chances on finding the way alone. Sometimes he ran into terrifying animals, with claws and pincers and gigantic jaws full of gleaming teeth, which they gnashed so loudly that they were audible from far in the distance. At these times, Eric flattened himself as much as possible against the wall to allow them to pass by. If they noticed him, Eric began very softly to hiss. If that didn't work, he would suddenly pull off his pajama top; he had discovered that this seemed to terrify the animals, and it was certainly easier than a fight, from which he would probably emerge the loser anyway.

Eric passed many hours under the ground in this manner. He had already noticed from the tiny holes above his head that the sun was about to set, when he at last made a fortunate encounter. A long, slippery earthworm crossed his path. The animal had suddenly stuck its head out of the wall a few steps ahead of where Eric was walking, waved it undecidedly back and forth a moment, and then bored determinedly into the wall on the opposite side. The passage of the long, thin body lasted several minutes and Eric could only stand uncomfortably by and watch. The last segment was about to disappear when he overcame his fear and shyly tapped on the end.

"Hey, what was that?" cried a frightened voice from deep in the earth.

"I beg your pardon," said Eric, squatting before the hole in the wall, "but I wanted to ask you something."

A pause followed, in which Eric could plainly hear the worm inch up a bit and then lie still. "Well, ask it then!" said the voice suspiciously.

"But am I not addressing the wrong end?" asked Eric. "Am I talking to your head or to the seat of your pants?"

"Oh, it all comes down to the same thing, as far as

that's concerned," said the voice. "I can talk and hear equally well with both ends." And, indeed, the voice suddenly sounded very close by.

Things are certainly strange in the insect world, thought Eric to himself. One constantly runs into the most peculiar things. Out loud he asked, "I would very much like to find the way out of here. Could you perhaps tell me how to do that?"

"Squirm," said the voice.

"What did you say?" asked Eric, who thought that he must have heard wrong.

"Squirm," repeated the worm. "You wait until it rains, and then you begin to squirm. The rest is easy." And he prepared to continue on his way.

"Oh please, sir," cried Eric into the hole, "wait a minute! I don't know how to squirm."

"Don't know how to squirm?" repeated the worm with surprise. "Well, what *do* you know how to do? Where were you brought up, anyway? I've never heard of a worm who didn't know how to squirm."

"But I'm not a worm at all!" cried Eric. "I'm a person!"

"A person," repeated the worm thoughtfully. "Never heard of it. What kind of an insect is that?"

"That is no kind of insect," said Eric. "A person is a human being, an erect-standing primate, gifted with reason and intelligence."

"Tut, tut, what a mouthful," mumbled the worm,

and Eric could hear him wriggle with irritation. "They all think they're hot stuff, but in the end, they're all for the worms. Now, what does a person look like?"

"But Mr. Worm," said Eric, "if you'll just come out, you can see for yourself."

"That won't help," answered the worm calmly, "because I don't have any eyes. So I can just as well stay here. Tell me what you look like and what kind of appendages you have. If you've got claws or pincers, then you can bet it will be a long time before I show myself. But if you're completely smooth, then there's no reason at all why I shouldn't show you the way."

"Well, to begin," said Eric, "we people have a head, in which one finds a mouth, a nose, two eyes, two ears—"

"All completely superfluous," broke in the worm. "But continue."

"Then comes the neck, of which nothing particular can be said—"

"That is just the most important part," interrupted the worm. "But go on."

"Then comes the torso."

"The what?"

"The torso," repeated Eric.

"What's that: the torso?"

"That is where the arms and legs are attached and—"

"Good heavens," said the worm. "Head, neck, torso, arms, legs—it's dizzying to listen to. Are you all

so complicated? And with all that, you still can't squirm?"

"No, I honestly can't," said Eric. "Not even if I do my best."

"Then I must ask myself what possible purpose all that extra baggage serves," continued the worm. "Throw that rubbish away and become a worm! How many legs do you have?"

"Two."

"That is two too many," sneered the worm, "although compared to the rest of the rabble that one encounters here, it's not all that bad."

"Thank you," said Eric. He was a bit insulted by "the rest of the rabble," but he needed the worm's help so he held his tongue.

"Two is actually the least that I have yet run into here, except of course, for my own family," said the worm. "I suspect that you are a worm-gone-wrong, or perhaps a worm-in-the-making."

"What is that? A worm-in-the-making?"

"A worm-in-the-making," said the worm, carefully bringing his front and back ends out of the hole (because he was beginning to trust Eric), "is a worm who has not yet become a worm, but for whom one may foster the hope that he will become one in the future. A caterpillar, for example, is a worm-in-the-making. He spins himself into a cocoon and does his utmost to lose all those ridiculous legs, but unfortunately it doesn't work. He turns into a butterfly. The effort is probably too much for him. There are other examples."

"But I have no intention of becoming a worm!" cried Eric. "It's never even occurred to me!"

"The instinct to improve oneself is inborn in everyone," said the worm. "One doesn't always have to consciously desire it. Without even having thought about it, it is quite possible that in the next minute you'll feel the need to spin yourself into a cocoon, and then there's no holding back. Let's suppose that happens, just for the fun of it. You're all wrapped up and you feel tired. You fall asleep. And when you wake up, you are a worm. I'm not promising anything, now. Remember that. I'm only saying that it's *possible*. Up till now, it has always been a butterfly or an ant or some such thing that appears. The leap seems to be too great. But in any case, your desire to squirm above and beyond, to reach for something higher, is a noble one, which I esteem. After all, one cannot do more than mean well; the rest is fate. But here we are!" The worm lay in a great pile on the ground and one end waved around helplessly in the air. "Where are you?" he asked. "In front, in back, or on the side?"

"Here, right next to you," said Eric. "A bit to your right. No, a bit further. Now you've got it." He shivered as the slimy animal groped at him.

"Your skin is awfully loose," said the worm after a while. "One would almost think that it was going to fall off at any minute."

"That it can," answered Eric. "The real skin is underneath."

"Just as I thought," said the worm with satisfaction. "You are shedding your skin, my good fellow. In a few days, it will all fall off and you'll be just like new." And the insect babbled on as it began to uncoil itself in order to show Eric the way.

"Usually," he said, "those who don't know the way keep following one of the rising paths to get outside, but they never make it. One must actually choose the down-sloping paths, which suddenly lead steeply upwards to the surface at their ends. That is a protective strategy. In case of danger, one can quickly hide one-self back deep in the ground. If, for example, there is a robin in the neighborhood. You've got to keep your wits about you at all times. Can you follow me?"

"You go rather fast around the curves," said Eric.

"No, I mean my reasoning," said the worm. "Were you able to follow my reasoning?"

"Oh definitely," said Eric. "That was clearly under-standable."

"Now that makes me very happy. If there's any-thing you don't understand, then don't be afraid to ask. I much prefer to have someone honestly say 'I don't understand,' than to have the feeling that I'm losing him. That's very unsettling. Watch out for this clump of earth; it's loose. Now, any questions?"

"Yes," said Eric, "but please don't get angry. You may think it odd."

"Come, come, come," said the worm, who now began to twist himself into the strangest shapes, "you don't have to be embarrassed. We can't all be worms. What is it?"

"Well, I just wondered . . ." Eric struggled to find the right words in order not to insult the worm. "I just wondered how you could be so — so cheerful, even though you're blind."

"I can understand your hesitation," said the worm, tying himself into yet another knot. "The question is indeed dumb. But that doesn't matter, because one learns from one's ignorance. The problem is that you've got things turned around in your head. It is a privilege to be blind. How many insects do you know who are blind? I can count the number on my segments, there are so few. We worms need no eyes. You do. It is a sign of weakness. You also need a head and arms and legs. You have become complicated out of helplessness. We don't need any of that. What would I do with arms and legs? What use do I have for eyes? Would I see anything that I don't already know?" And the worm chattered on like that, tying himself up in ever more complicated knots out of sheer pleasure.

"Watch out," Eric interrupted more than once. "You'll never get untangled!" But the worm paid no attention to this warning and by the time he had finished his speech, he was tightly stuck in a large knot.

"Now you've done it!" cried Eric. "Let's see you get out of that one!"

The worm writhed and twisted in all directions, only tying himself still tighter. "Give me a hand!" he cried, panting. "Don't just stand there gawking!"

"No, I'm keeping out of it," said Eric, eyeing the slimy mass with disgust. "Do it yourself!"

"But I can't see anything!" cried the worm. "I haven't the faintest idea where the knots are. You at least have eyes in your head!"

"Try it yourself first," said Eric, sitting down on a pebble at the side of the passage, "and if that doesn't work, then we'll see what's next." He wrapped his right hand in his handkerchief in anticipation of having to help the slimy beast out of his predicament. Eric found him truly repulsive, but felt too sorry for him to walk off and leave him in such a state. The worm, in the meantime, was doing his best to create order out of chaos. But he just pulled all of the old knots even tighter and then added a few new ones to boot. When finally he couldn't move even a single segment of his body, he started to cry.

"Oh, please help me," he sobbed. "I'm totally confused. I don't even know where to begin anymore. Where are my ends? Can you see them?"

"Yes, I can. *I* have eyes in my head," muttered Eric disgustedly, coming closer. "But the question is: how do I get this mess untangled? There is no place to get a grip. Bah, what an unappetizing job! Well, let's give it a try." He half closed his eyes and waded bravely in. But even though he did his best, Eric was unable to get anywhere. The poor dumb animal didn't understand him, and every time Eric got a loop free, the worm just tangled it up again. Eric was about to give up and go for help, when he heard a voice behind him.

"Somebody have an accident?"

It was an ant who asked.

CHAPTER ELEVEN

The ant had been carrying a huge white ball on his shoulders which he now set down in order to better inspect the situation. "He's gotten himself into a pretty fix!" said the ant, shaking his head as he viewed the spectacle of the worm. "Relative of yours?"

Eric dried his hands and introduced himself.

"Pinksterblom!" repeated the ant with surprise. "Are you the famous Pinksterblom? The whole neighborhood's talking about you. One hears the most incredible stories." The ant stepped back a few paces in order to better observe Eric. "One thing is true at any rate," he said. "You do indeed walk on two legs. Well, well, what a surprise! Everyone has something to say about you. One hears *this* from the wasps and *that* from the butterflies. They all contradict each other. One says that you are extremely erudite, and the other that you are as dumb as an ox. What is one to believe?"

"I'm hardly erudite, but neither am I so dumb,"

said Eric, blushing at being the center of so much attention. "I was only good in Botany—and for that I had an A before the vacation. The rest were all B's and C's."

"Not so bad," said the ant, who didn't want to let on that he didn't understand a single word of it. "Do you know what this is?" he asked, indicating the longish white object which he had just set down.

"An ant egg," said Eric.

"Wrong!" cried the ant triumphantly. "The usual mistake! It's an ant larva. It would have been quite a surprise if you had known it. Everyone makes the same mistake—even the birds who gobble them up think that they're eggs." The ant laughed heartily at the world's ignorance.

"That may be," said Eric, "but I find it more regrettable that what they eat is a larva than had it been an egg. A larva is more valuable. More time has gone into it."

"Do you think so?" asked the ant, suddenly serious. "I've never looked at it like that. Oh, dear!" He was wrapped up in thought and looked with concern at the white object that had been entrusted to his keeping. "My assignment is to set this larva in the sun," he said. "It is almost ready to hatch. But if you think it's safer to wait until dark when the birds have gone to bed—"

"But then the sun is also gone," said Eric. "Surely you see that."

"Oh, dear!" muttered the ant. "Life can be so diffi-

cult if you think about it. If there's sun, then there are
birds; and if there are no birds, then neither is there any
sun!"

"But you don't *have* to think about it," said Eric.
"Only people have to think. You just *do*. We are the
ones who need *Solm's.*"

"Exactly, *Solm's,*" repeated the ant. "That is the
word in everyone's mouth these days. What does
Solm's say in this case?"

"I wouldn't dream of telling you," answered Eric
with determination. "I wish I had never mentioned
Solm's to anyone here. Now all you poor insects can't
do anything anymore without wondering what *Solm's*
has to say about it."

"Wondering?" cried the ant. "That's putting it
mildly! No one gets a wink of sleep anymore. If you'll
come outside with me, then you'll see something!

Among us, the ants, everything is in utter confusion. Everyone is waiting for your arrival, to hear how things should go!"

"But that's *awful!*" cried Eric in turn. "The whole world's falling apart. Take me there immediately."

"Fine," said the ant, "but what am I to do with the larva? Should I set it in the sun, or should I leave it here, or — "

"Tell me," said Eric, "what did you intend to do with it before you met me?"

"I was going to bring it outside and set it in the sun."

"Well, do just that. That's perfect. And I'll go with you. I must set things straight without delay!"

"And what about me?" called the worm. "Must I stay here tied up in knots?"

"I'll come back with help," promised Eric. "I can't do it alone. Now listen: what is the diameter of a circle that can fit inside a square with a diagonal length of x?"

"I don't get you," said the worm, puzzled.

"It's a riddle," said Eric. "You must try to figure it out while I'm gone. The time will go faster that way. Now, good-bye, Mr. Worm. As soon as I've found help, I'll be back to unknot you. Till then." Eric waved, nodded encouragement, and was off. He marched straight ahead after the ant without looking around until he saw the first rays of light before them.

Oh, how happy he was to see the sun again and the blue sky!

But as soon as he stepped out into the fading sunlight, he was approached from all sides by a multitude of insects loaded down with eggs and larvae, all clamoring for his advice.

"Mr. Pinksterblom! Mr. Pinksterblom! Come and take a look at this!"

"Are these eggs good?"

"When will they hatch?"

"Should I lay them in the sun or in the shade?"

There was such pushing and shoving and shouting that it was impossible to see or hear anything clearly.

A young praying mantis mother held an emaciated larva up before his eyes. "Mr. Pinksterblom," she pleaded, "please have a look! He seems so weak. I didn't dare give him anything to eat before asking you. What must I do for him?"

"Ladies, ladies," called Eric, who saw in an instant that they were all mothers, "if you wait to ask me, then everything can only go wrong. I know very little, and I should have kept silent about that bit. Left to yourselves, you do everything precisely as it stands in *Solm's*. I have even observed that you often do it better. I don't know how that can be, I only know that it is. Go back to your work and do it as you feel it should be done, as you have always done it. If you feel the urge to lay forty eggs, then by all means, do so. Don't ask yourself: is that not a bit extravagant? Is such a pile perhaps a little crazy? What would *Solm's* have to say about this? Because everything that you do is exactly as described in *Solm's,* and if it is described differently there, then it is Solm who is mistaken, not you. And now, Mrs. Mantis, what do you usually feed your larva?"

"Leaf lice," whispered the lady, "but I'm not sure——"

"You needn't have any doubts," interrupted Eric. "Leaf lice——excellent! That is precisely what he needs, the little rascal." He tickled the little larva under the chin and turned his attention to a June bug who stood nearby with a worried expression on her face. "What is it, ma'am? Can I help you?"

"I can't tell you in public," she whispered.

"Then let's step aside here, behind this fern. Now, what is it?"

"I'm going to lay some eggs," she whispered, "this afternoon, I think."

"Good," said Eric. "Don't try to stop it."

"No, I can't stop it," answered the bug. "I just want to do it right. I've been so nervous since I heard that it's all been written up in a book."

"I'm sure you'll do fine."

"It's just that I have such a strange number in my head. I don't want to shock you."

"What is it?" asked Eric. "I'll bet it's exactly right."

"Eighty," whispered the June bug, her head bowed.

"You see!" cried Eric. "Precisely what *Solm's* says!"

"You don't think it's a bit much?"

"For myself, actually, yes," answered Eric truthfully. "A chicken lays only one egg. But it's just right for you, all the same. You're no chicken, after all."

"And should I sit next to them? Or on top of them? Or should I simply lay them in the sun? Or does *Solm's* say—"

"Don't give *Solm's* another thought," Eric broke in decidedly. "Don't give anything another thought. Don't think at all. Once the eggs have arrived, you'll see how easy it all is. You'll even do the things in the small print as if you were born to them. You *were* born to them! You know it far better than *Solm's*—that's the miracle of nature. Now, chin up, ma'am, and give my best to the youngsters!"

It's just awful, thought Eric to himself as he headed back to the ant. Everything is in total confusion. No one dares to do anything on his own anymore.

"It's just as bad with us," said the ant, as though reading his thoughts. "Everyone is awaiting your arrival. Not a single egg has been laid and the larvae lie around everywhere waiting to be carried into the sun. A couple of the old workers have steadfastly continued feeding the larvae, but we're not at all sure if that's good."

"Good gracious," muttered Eric. "Quickly, quickly, where is the anthill?"

"Over there! That's it!"

"Let's run, then," cried Eric. "Maybe we're still in time. Put that larva down!"

"Where?"

"Just put it down!" shouted Eric impatiently.

"Is this good?" asked the ant, propping the larva against a blade of grass and looking inquiringly at Eric.

"Goodness gracious!" cried Eric, stamping with impatience. "What is wrong with all these insects? It's enough to try a saint. Let the thing lay there and stop agonizing. It's fine! Now, hold your tongue and run!" And off they sped, as fast as they could go.

"Mr. Pinksterblom! Mr. Pinksterblom!" called a voice.

"Oh, what is it now?" cried Eric, still running but looking around. "A spider," said the ant, his stinger at the ready, "just above your head."

Eric looked up and saw a painfully thin garden spider in a half-finished web.

"Are you the famous Mr. Pinksterblom?" she asked. "The one who knows everything?"

"Oh, sure," grumbled the ant. " 'Everything' is a bit strong. He certainly didn't know about the ant larva. Take care, Mr. Pinksterblom, spiders are a dangerous sort, they flatter and coax, and before you know it, you're trapped."

"Yes, I know them well," answered Eric, taking a few steps backward. "What's wrong, ma'am?"

"Suddenly, I don't know anything anymore," complained the spider. "Should I go left or right? Am I

using the right thread? Are the lines close enough together?"

"You've all gone crazy!" cried Eric angrily. "I'm not
saying another word. You're all asking what you already know."

"Yes, but have I got the pattern right?" asked the
spider, anxiously pacing back and forth. "Is the glue
perhaps too thick?"

"Just keep going," advised Eric, who could still feel
sympathy for the confused creature. "The glue is perfect and the pattern is extremely tasteful. It's only a
shame that it's not for a better purpose."

"That last got her," said the ant with satisfaction as
they ran farther. "Every last one of those bloodsuckers
should be wiped out, if you ask me. What does *Solm's*
say?"

"According to *Solm's*, they're very useful," said Eric.
"They catch flies and mosquitoes and all kinds of other
pests."

"An uncle of mine was also caught in such a trap,"
said the ant. "It was the mating season and he was flying around like a lunatic. You know how it is when
someone's in love. He wasn't looking and he flew right
into the web. We heard him screaming for an hour before he was finally still." Eric had to dry his eyes with
his handkerchief, he was so touched.

"Yes, there is plenty of sorrow in the world," said
the ant, "and he was such a happy-go-lucky guy. The
evening before, he lay in his bed singing and whistling

162

and slapping the blankets and shouting, 'Tomorrow I'll be a father! Tomorrow I'll be a father!' And when tomorrow arrived, there he was, a dried-out shell, lying on the ground."

"Don't go on," sobbed Eric, "I can't take it anymore. I've never in my life heard such a sad story."

But just then they were interrupted by a shout from the sentry. "Password?!"

"Work!" replied the ant.

"And you?"

"I'm Mr. Pinksterblom," said Eric shyly.

"Oh, I beg your pardon," said the sentry, stepping aside immediately. "Enter!" And stepping into the anthill, Eric was met by the welcoming shouts of hundreds of ants.

CHAPTER TWELVE

This was a happy time for Eric, especially after all the hardships he had been through. He grew to know the diligent, hard-working life that went on from morning to night in the anthill under the pine needles, and he took great pleasure in sauntering around with his hands in his pockets, inspecting the activities of the busy ants. He was listened to with respect wherever he went, even though he limited his observations to saying that all was going as it should and that one must simply keep on at one's work. "I leave it to you," he answered repeatedly when asked something. "Keep it up! It's going great!" Then he nodded encouragingly and wandered farther. Gradually everything returned to normal for these busy insects and everyone leaned into his tasks with great enthusiasm.

There is plenty to be done in an orderly ant colony and Eric saw with his own eyes how just it is that ants are so often used as good examples for people. They dragged bales of food four times their own weight at a fast clip down into the cellar, and when one bale was delivered, they spat quickly in the palms of their hands and headed off for another. "Step aside, Mr. Pinksterblom," rang out constantly from all sides and Eric had to keep a careful lookout to be sure he wasn't trampled underfoot.

In the nursery it was much quieter and Eric liked standing there watching. Scarcely a moment passed when at least a few eggs didn't hatch, and he found it pleasant to watch the surprised expressions of the little larvae as they first faced the world. Immediately, one of the worker ants would rush over and stuff the newcomer full of as much honey as he had with him. "Careful, he'll burst!" cried Eric now and then, but there was apparently no danger. The little ones just stretched their horny jaws open that much wider and waited silently for more.

Eric, as a male, was not allowed in the area where the eggs were laid, but he made himself very useful, transporting the freshly produced larvae. He carried great baskets full, as though they weighed nothing, up the ladders to the outdoors and set them down neatly next to each other in the sun. He did break one or two once in a while, but no one seemed to mind. Only one time, when he let an entire basket fall, did they look surprised and ask if that was also from *Solm's*.

Eric's happiness was interrupted one day by a thought of the earthworm. He had almost forgotten the beast's unfortunate situation, when suddenly, while watching the leaf lice, he remembered the poor blind animal. A moment later, a small army of worker ants came marching down the hill, and Eric promptly sent them off in the name of *Solm's* to rescue his former acquaintance.

Bursting with impatience, Eric waited for them to return, and when he finally spotted them in the distance, he ran down the hill to meet them. But the sight that greeted him brought tears to his eyes. Every ant, followed in line by one of his fellows, carried a single segment of worm in his jaws, and the poor thing was set down in front of him in a hundred pieces.

"But that's not at all what I meant!" cried Eric. "I asked you to untangle him!"

"And? Here he is, untangled," replied the leader. There wasn't much more to be said.

"Did he say anything?" asked Eric. "A last word?"

"Actually, yes, but we didn't understand it. It seemed to be the solution to a riddle."

"Oh, gosh, yes, that's just what it was!" said Eric sadly, and the tears rolled down his cheeks. "I'd given him a riddle to solve to pass the time."

"I have the part with the mouth," said one of the ants, coming forward with his piece of worm. "It has done nothing but babble nonsense the entire trip. Perhaps you'd care to listen?"

"Ha, Mr. Pinksterblom!" cried the segment. "Is that finally you? Will you please tell this gentleman to put me down *immediately*—if not sooner!"

"Still the same," said Eric sadly. "You've had it, Mr. Worm! They've simply cut the knot; you've been chopped up into a hundred pieces."

"Good grief," muttered the segment, "that is unexpected news. Give me a moment to let it sink in. A hundred pieces, you say? Is that fatal, Mr. Pinksterblom?"

"Yes, I believe so," said Eric, considering. "In any event, it is very serious."

"I was afraid so," mumbled the segment. "I felt so faint, as though I was missing something. And how is it with the others?"

"Most of them aren't even moving any more," said Eric, looking around.

"Lucky that I can't see anything," said the segment with an ever-weakening voice. "Unhappy animals who can see . . . Good day, Mr. Pinksterblom . . ." And with that, he breathed his last.

"You'll find," said a wise old ant, to whom Eric had told the entire story of the worm as they headed back to the anthill, "that it's always those whom you'd least expect that have the most imagination. What was the answer to the riddle?"

"I don't know," said Eric. "It was just something to keep his mind off his problems."

"Oh," said the ant, "I guess it really doesn't matter after all, does it?"

We now look in on the great feast that was to be given

that evening in Eric's honor. He had magnanimously offered the remains of the worm for a culinary extravaganza, and all day long the mouth-watering aroma of barbecuing filled every passage of the anthill. "It's going to be extraordinary," they all agreed, and even the smallest larvae who had just struggled out of their eggs looked forward to a gastronomic experience to remember. There were all kinds of other preparations underway, but Eric was unable to discover the cause of all the whispering that he encountered at every bustling center of activity.

"They're learning a song written in your honor," confided one of the ants to him, no longer able to keep the secret. "It's going to be a jubilee cantata for eight voices."

"Good heavens," mumbled Eric.

"It's fantastic," continued the ant, letting the cat completely out of the bag. "I've heard the beginning, and I can assure you, I've never heard anything so moving. It goes straight to your heart."

"Oh, but they mustn't do that," said Eric bashfully. "I'm just a little boy, and they are all full-grown ants. It's just not proper."

"I don't see why not," said the ant. "You are a scholar. You know exactly what is inside an egg before it even hatches, and that counts much more than years. And besides, every ant likes to party now and then. No, you certainly mustn't think it improper."

But Eric hurried off to talk to the conductor, who

was just beginning to rehearse another section with a
group of crickets. Like all great musicians, he had let
his antennae grow out to a wild, unkempt coiffure,
and he stamped his feet and jumped around and
waved his forelegs furiously in all directions at once.

"Excuse me, but may I interrupt a moment?" asked
Eric shyly.

"For Pete's sake, what is it now?" cried the conductor, spinning around with eyes afire. "Oh, pardon me,
Mr. Pinksterblom, how may I be of service to you?"

Eric respectfully laid out his objections to a song in
his honor.

"Hmm," said the conductor, after he had sent the

crickets away. "Modesty is a commendable attribute, but you must nonetheless try to overcome it, Mr. Pinksterblom. You have, after all, provided the worm. People have occasionally given a leaf louse in the past, and once, even a caterpillar — but a worm! There is only one fitting answer: a cantata."

"Well, I'm very honored," said Eric. "Did you write it?"

"The music is mine," answered the conductor, smiling, "but not the words. Just between the two of us, Mr. Pinksterblom, the lyrics are wretched. No form, no content — not a single uplifting thought. That's dumped in your lap and you have to set it to music. I tell you! One does one's best, but . . ." and the great artist sunk silently into pained thought.

"I'm terribly sorry," began Eric.

"Oh, it's nothing," continued the ant, with a consolatory smile. "Later, when one is dead, people begin to appreciate one. But not while one is alive. They aren't ready for it."

"Not ready for what?" asked Eric.

"For my music. It's way over their heads. They pretend to understand it, but they don't really hear a single note." The maestro shook his head and smiled sadly.

"Gee, that's awful," said Eric. "Have you written very much of that incomprehensible music?"

"Not much," said the artist, "but all profound pieces. My three string quartets, for example. Each one a masterpiece, if I do say so myself. And then there's my milking song, to be sung during the milking of leaf lice. And, of course, my unforgettable egg song."

"And what is that?" asked Eric.

"The egg song must be sung by the mothers at the moment that they lay an egg. At least, that was the intention. But do you think that anyone does it? Not a solitary soul."

"Maybe they're too busy at the time," suggested Eric.

"Nonsense," said the ant. "That is precisely why I wrote the song: to help them relax. Sheer slackness, lack of initiative. And my other egg song, to be sung as the eggs hatch."

"By whom?" asked Eric, in amazement.

"By the hatchlings, of course," answered the composer. "Don't you find it a delightful thought, that the first thing a newborn would do when he entered the world is sing a song, a hymn to nature? But do you think that any of them does it? Not one!"

"But they couldn't possibly ever have heard about it," said Eric.

"Excuses," said the ant. "And I have worked the sound of cracking eggshells so masterfully into the piece. One hears the eggs. I could even say, one sees them before one's very eyes. It is a mighty epic, sir, a mighty epic! The melody begins slow and heavy and you feel, as it were, that here we have an unhatched egg. Then you hear a gentle cracking, getting louder and louder. And then, the end! With what can I best compare the end?''

"With an empty eggshell?'' suggested Eric.

"That's it,'' confirmed the composer, "with a completely empty eggshell. A wind-egg, one could almost say. Don't you think it's tremendous? But now I must go back to work: the ladies' choir is waiting to rehearse the sixth voice. Mr. Pinksterblom, until this evening.'' And he strode away.

Eric was still somewhat uncomfortable that such an extraordinary artist was making so tremendous an effort on his behalf, and he waited anxiously for the evening meal to begin. But it all turned out much better than he had expected. The atmosphere was friendly and relaxed. The large dining room was cheerfully decorated and little fireflies flickered on and off, providing the lighting. The table was beautifully set and a delicious piece of worm lay on each plate. They had even been thoughtful enough to cook something different for Eric, since he had been friendly with the source of the main dish. On his plate was a roasted leaf louse and an omelet of broken ant eggs. His chair was also set a bit higher than the others and decorated with leaves.

It was a charming meal, and Eric found it especially nice that he didn't constantly have to keep the conversation going. His table partner on one side was a lady who every now and then had to excuse herself to go lay an egg, and on the other side of him sat an old gentle-

174

man who babbled on and on without pausing for breath, and was too deaf in one ear to understand much of what was said anyway. He looked very surprised when Eric, after having carefully studied him for a while, suddenly said, "You are a bachelor, I see."

"But Mr. Pinksterblom," answered the gentleman, amazed, "how did you know that?"

"I'll tell you," said Eric. "Among the ants, the men always die as soon as they get married. That also happens with bees, actually, but we haven't studied them yet. You are still alive, so you must not be married."

"Exactly so," confirmed the ant, blushing. "And don't you find it actually quite unreasonable? Look at all those proper young ants. Consider, for example, that young fellow across the table from us. He works and he slaves and within a week, he's a goner."

"Yes," agreed Eric, "it does seem a shame."

At that moment one of the ants stood up and cleared his throat. A deep, respectful silence immediately filled the room. It was the oldest member of the colony present, an ancient, gray worker. He raised his wavering voice and gave such an eloquent and moving speech that tears rolled helplessly down the cheeks of everyone in the room. He painted the joy of the mothers at the hatching of the eggs, and the honorable calling of fatherhood, which claimed the lives of those who so nobly gave themselves up to it. A sigh filled the air. The speaker continued: he himself had experienced neither one nor the other — he could only describe what he had seen. He was simply a worker — not a "he" or a "she" — just an "it." But exactly because of this neutrality, he felt himself in a position to observe life impartially. He had observed it long and closely and he was convinced that he could honestly say that life is beautiful (applause). Not that there weren't occasional setbacks. On the contrary. The disaster of the previous year, when a bristly beast — Mr. Pinksterblom perhaps can tell us the name?

"A hedgehog," said Eric (warm applause).

When a hedgehog marauded through the nursery, greedily slurping up 573 ant larvae and leaving the young colony on the brink of extinction, was still all too clear in his mind. He also remembered the terrible battle with the red ants this past spring that had cost the lives of 150 female and 348 worker ants.

"May I interrupt a moment?" asked one of the male ants, getting to his feet. "I wouldn't want Mr. Pinksterblom to get the wrong impression of us males. We weren't around yet when that happened."

"Yes, I know," answered Eric. "Males aren't born until the fall."

A whisper of admiration passed through the company, and it was a minute or two before the speaker could continue. He apologized for his forgetfulness: the males were indeed not yet here, and had they been, they would most certainly have fought bravely to the last man for the fatherland (applause). As it was, the honor fell that time to the women and the workers, who are actually better equipped by nature for the task.

"Why is that?" whispered Eric, surprised.

"Because we have stingers," whispered the lady next to him, "and those good-for-nothings don't."

The speaker asked not to have to describe the battle in all its particulars. The memories associated with it were still too fresh and painful and this was, after all, a celebration. He wished, however, to pay tribute to all those who had fallen and he asked everyone present to stand for a minute of silence.

They all stood up and stared at their plates. One could hear a pin drop, it was so still. Only the crack of hatching eggs from the nursery could be heard.

When the minute was up, the speaker tapped on his glass and said that he would like to sound a few happier notes. There were many, but he wanted to keep it short (thankful applause).

"Whenever are we going to eat?" complained Eric in a whisper. "My leaf louse is getting cold."

"Oh, he's far from finished," whispered his tablemate. "He does this at every party. Those old workers can be a sore trial for us all."

There was, in the first place, the high birth rate of recent months that the speaker announced with satisfaction. The ladies could look back on more than 3,000 eggs hatched. He praised all those involved in the effort. There were indeed a few casualties (laughter and smiles in Eric's direction), and once even a whole basket was dropped (more laughter — Eric blushed deep red), but when the tree is so laden with fruit, one doesn't miss one or two of the apples. The deficit was quickly made up. As far as the larvae were concerned, the colony was no less fortunate. The night frost had indeed taken its toll, but overall, one had reason to be satisfied.

A pleasant surprise this year was the rich harvest in leaf lice. The food cellars were full and the colony could look forward to a winter of plenty.

But the greatest fortune and the highest honor that had been bestowed on the colony this year was the presence in their midst of a creature surpassing in knowledge and modesty, miraculous in physical form, still more astounding in mental abilities and blessed with the gifts of prophecy and foresight. In short, Mr. Pinksterblom (hearty cheers and clapping, growing into a standing ovation).

Eric stood up and bowed in every direction and then sat down again in confusion. I wish everyone at home could see this, he thought to himself as the cheering continued.

When all was finally quiet again, the speaker continued. As an old man with his two hind legs already in the grave, who this year most likely would not wake up again out of his winter sleep, he could be permitted to say this: he had thought, till now, that he knew a thing or two. He had, before meeting Mr. Pinksterblom, believed himself to possess a certain amount of

knowledge and experience. He knew now that he knew nothing (applause). He was just a muddler (warm applause). And from what he could see, all the other ants were also just muddlers (less enthusiastic applause). The only one who really knew anything was Mr. Pinksterblom. It was no shame to feel oneself ignorant compared to such a being. Mr. Pinksterblom had once, for example, explained to him in great detail why the larvae must be laid out in the sun, and he had stood dumbfounded by the wisdom that ruled in nature. Knowledge is power; since he had learned that everything had a reason, he had worked with redoubled fire to bring the larvae up into the sun. Indeed, he had managed to increase his rate from twelve to fourteen larvae transported per hour (applause).

The speaker had often wondered to which animal type Mr. Pinksterblom actually belonged, and he was not the only one. As an old ant, he could say it straight out. It was the question of the day, and he had been asked dozens of times to touch on this point in his speech. He did it with great hesitation, but he was overcome by curiosity. Must he enter his grave without ever knowing the answer? Would Mr. Pinksterblom perhaps be willing to reveal this secret to the present company at this time?

"I'll do my best," said Eric. "I just hope you're not all disappointed."

"It couldn't possibly disappoint us," said the ant.

"Well, then," said Eric blushing, "I am a person." Immediately, a deafening cheer broke loose and it was only too clear that with these words, a long and strained tension had been released.

"A person!" cried the speaker. "Wonderful! A person! I ask you all to drink a toast to the health and prosperity of these intelligent insects!"

Eric clinked glasses with perhaps a thousand others, and then remained standing, looking around in embarrassment and confusion.

"You must respond!" whispered the lady next to him.

But Eric sat down in his chair and began to cry! Everyone was thoroughly disconcerted. "But Mr. Pinksterblom!" they all cried.

"He's getting a stinger," suggested the old ant next to Eric.

"Quiet!" shouted the worker ant. "Quiet everyone! What's wrong, Mr. Pinksterblom?"

"Oh, I'm so terribly homesick," sobbed Eric. "I don't belong here at all! I've already been wandering around for three weeks in my pajamas and I just can't seem to find the picture frame. What must they be saying at home? And what can be happening with Polly?"

"Yes, his stinger is coming through," mumbled the old gentleman, shaking his head.

"Quiet!" called the worker ant. "We don't understand you, Mr. Pinksterblom. Are you speaking poetically? What do you mean by the picture frame? And who is . . . who is —"

"Polly," said Eric, drying his tears. "That was my pet mouse."

A tremor went through the entire ant colony. "A mouse, sir?" cried the worker, clutching fast to the table with fright. "Where have you left the beast?"

"Beast?" cried Eric, sobbing heavily again at the thought of his pet. "She never hurt anyone. When I first brought her home from the pet shop, she was barely an inch long, and now she's almost as big as my pinky. When I called her, she would pop out from under her cedar shavings all by herself." The memories were too much for him and he burst into fresh tears.

"It's his stinger, all right," insisted the old ant. "In a few minutes it will all be over."

"Ladies and gentlemen," said the worker ant in a solemn tone, "I am of another opinion. I have observed our honored guest carefully in recent times and I believe that he has yet another secret. Sometimes I saw him sunk in thought beside a basket of larvae, and a few times I even saw him wipe away a tear as he carried them into the sun. His conversation, especially when it concerns sizes and weights, is often so extraordinary that I found myself wondering: does Mr. Pinksterblom really come from Industrious Valley? I have never broached this subject with anyone. Mr. Pinksterblom is entirely free to reveal his origins or not, as he will. But if something is bothering him, then I say, unburden yourself, Mr. Pinksterblom! Let us share your secret! Maybe we can help you. Five thousand is better than one, even if that one is a Pinksterblom. And if it comes to a fight, my stinger is ready!"

Rarely had a speech been greeted with such an emotional response. A high, shrill buzz filled the room: it was the battle hymn of the ants, and it sounded from five thousand throats at once. Everyone stood at attention with shining eyes, and those with stingers held them at the ready. The words of the war song burst out:

Advance! Advance!
That is our decision!

We are no longer ants,
But insects of vision!
Hold your stinger high!
We're off to do or die!

"Oh, no," cried Eric, laughing through his tears, "there's really nothing wrong! If you'll all sit down, I'll tell you how I got here. It is surely one of the strangest stories that you'll ever hear. Shall I begin?"

Everyone sat down and listened in breathless silence to Eric's tale.

CHAPTER THIRTEEN

The next day, Eric marched out at the head of the troops, and anything that could in any sense be called an ant marched out in close drill behind him. Everyone was curious to see if it was possible to climb over the frame to the other side. In the excitement of the evening before, Eric had gotten carried away in his speech and invited all the ants to his house. "Everyone will be warmly welcome," he had exclaimed. "There is room for everyone who wants to come. I'll see to it that there is a dish of fresh food ready every morning, and I'll warn my brothers to watch where they are walking. No one will have to work anymore, and if anyone gets sick, I'll call the vet."

"Mr. Pinksterblom," the old worker ant had answered on everyone's behalf, "you are too good. We scarcely dare to accept your invitation. Don't you think it will be too much work for your mother?"

"Oh, my mother loves to have company," Eric had replied.

Then there was no stopping them! Everyone had jumped up from the table and begun to get ready for the trip. Eric had never seen such industry! The whole night long, he heard sounds of the sharpening of stingers, the cries of the workers who were bringing the eggs and larvae to safety in the cellars, and the dragging of clumps of earth to close off the entrances for three weeks.

The sight of all these preparations was somewhat unsettling to Eric. Where will I put them all? he wondered secretly to himself, a bit too late. And will they feel at home in our house after all?

But when he pictured himself at the head of all those ants entering the living room and marching three times around the table before the eyes of his amazed relatives, this vision chased away all of his misgivings and he even pitched in to help with everything that needed to be done before the departure. The sun was scarcely above the horizon when everyone filed out the remaining exit in a long line into the clear, crisp air.

It was a magnificent morning! The new day unfolded in flaming red and orange, and all the vegetation that had been bowed under by the weight of the last dewdrops straightened up and shook off its watery fleece like a diamond cape.

"Nature always makes one feel so uplifted," said Eric, looking joyfully around, "and rarely disappoints the observant traveler." This was a sentence out of his French conversation book; it stood between parentheses since it was actually meant for more advanced students.

"So true," said the ant who was walking next to him. "You have hit the nail on the head."

"Aren't we going to sing?" asked Eric. "That would be so cheerful now. Last evening — "

Even before he could finish, the first strains of the war song could be heard from the farthest ranks, and immediately, everyone joined in:

> *Advance! Advance!*
> *That is our decision!*
> *We are no longer ants,*
> *But insects of vision!*
> *Hold your stinger high!*
> *We're off to do or die!*

The song resounded in the quiet morning right to the tops of the mole hills, and it caused a terrible panic in those insects who chanced to be in the area. Without stopping to look around, they all ran like mad for shelter, and the snails dropped out of the grass to the ground like acorns out of oak trees.

"Couldn't we sing a little more quietly?" Eric asked his companions. "We're scaring everyone to death!"

"That's just the fun of it!" said one of the ants, standing on his back legs and rubbing his hands together with satisfaction. But even so short a pause proved fatal. The ant was immediately trampled underfoot, without the slightest halt in the singing, and when Eric walked around to the back of the column to see if anything remained of his late comrade, there was nothing left to be found.

"Life is hard," agreed several of the oldsters who were bringing up the rear, "life is hard. But you are about to experience something truly worth living for. Fighting, stinging, and biting! Fantastic!"

Eric, who had been so happy all this time thinking that he had at last found a group of insects who seemed to understand the limitations of their world, and even longed for wider horizons, suddenly began to harbor suspicions about the actual aim of the trip. Before he could give voice to these thoughts, an angry buzz filled the air, and he was pushed aside by a horde of furiously advancing ants.

"What's wrong?" he cried, remaining upright with difficulty.

"A worm," answered an old ant who stood next to him watching the struggle. "And what a worm!" Her eyes sparkled. "Are they so big and fat on your side too, Mr. Pinksterblom?" she asked.

The uneven match was quickly over. What otherwise might have been a whole day's provisions for a nest of baby robins was torn apart and gulped down by the ants in the wink of an eye. And the carnage didn't stop there. Far from it! The troops advanced voraciously, devouring everything in their path, and leaving a trail of broken eggs, crippled wings, and discarded legs behind. The mournful cries of the terrified survivors could be heard everywhere. Eric, disconsolately bringing up the rear guard, came across a family of centipedes that had been totally disjointed. The mother sat dejectedly among her shattered eggs, mourning for her larvae, every last one of which was gone.

"And we hadn't done anything, Mr. Pinksterblom, nothing at all," sobbed the unhappy mother. As for father centipede, he sat silently in his chair and said nothing: his head had been bitten off!

"Something has got to be done!" said Eric. "This was not my intention at all!" And he ran like the wind to the front of the army of ants, jumping over branches and roots, to bring the attackers to reason. But when he had overtaken the leaders, he saw a strange phenomenon: motionless and silent, they all stood drawn up in battle order. He could not remember ever having seen the ants so serious. Each one stood in the line next to his neighbor, staring ahead with shining eyes and not moving.

"Shhh!" whispered the ant whom Eric had asked to enlighten him about the situation. "Look straight ahead of you." Eric stood up on his tiptoes and peered over the heads in front of him. There, not a hundred steps away, stood another ant army, also ranged in battle order. Eric could see their sharpened stingers clearly. They weren't black, like their opponents, but reddish-brown, and considerably more robust of build.

They were led by a giant of an ant, who was missing one eye, and who every now and then spat on the ground to show his contempt. For a long time, this was the only movement in the field.

Eric wondered to himself where all this was leading, when suddenly an ear-splitting shout filled the air. He received a blow to his back, then two more in his side, and was driven forward like a top by the battling throng. It was a terrible fight! The enemies ripped off each other's legs and bit off each other's heads as though it was the most usual thing in the world. And although none of it all was really Eric's business, he found himself gradually drawn in by the excitement. His breath came faster and faster, and suddenly he laid into the nearest red contenders in the field with clenched fists. "Bravo, Mr. Pinksterblom!" he heard all around him. "Let 'em have it!"

What happened after that he could never exactly say for certain; he was overcome by a wild passion. Blindly, he snatched at a back leg from out of the fray, and swung it in a furious circle around his head like a lunatic, striking fear and terror into the enemy's heart. He fought like a Fury. He was just about to deliver another crushing blow somewhere, when a stream of sharp, biting dampness was sprayed in his face. He knew instantly that this was the fearsome ant acid, and he sat down immediately on the ground, rubbing his stinging eyes.

As he rubbed and rubbed, he felt something strange

happening to him. It was as though he was getting bigger and bigger, and when he finally dared to take a peek around, he saw that he was sitting up in his own bed, in his own room, with both fists rubbing his eyes.

The sun shone through the slit in the curtains, and the light was so bright that he had to lie back on his pillow. He was infinitely surprised. He remained lying with his nose above the blanket for a while, looking around the room. It was precisely as it was when he had left it. The warm sun glowed through the red curtains, and the birds chirped outside in the garden. Eric listened to the cheerful sounds, and suddenly he was as happy as could be. He slipped out of bed, and the next minute he was leaning over the windowsill, looking outside.

Everything looked so wonderfully fresh in the early

morning light. The damp grass steamed in the glow of the rising sun as though the garden had lain in a bath the whole previous evening. A cloud of fine mist rose from the glistening leaves of the two pear trees. In the distance, a little girl waved from her balcony and Eric waved back with joy. A moment ago, still in bed, he had thought that perhaps he had awakened inside a flower blossom, or in one of the many rooms of The Snail Shell. But now he recognized everything clearly: the brown fence around the neighbor's garden, the old, black shovel in the dirt pile, the sandbox without sand, the leaning gazebo, and the little girl on the balcony.

When Eric finally pulled his head back inside, everything seemed suddenly darker. He pulled the curtains open, and examined all the portraits in the room closely. But not a single one said a word. Even Grandma Pinksterblom seemed not to recognize him and remained sitting motionless in her rocker, with her hands in her lap.

It's a bit strange, thought Eric to himself. How come they never want to have anything to do with me once it's light out?

He pondered for a moment, and then decided to surprise his family with his sudden entrance as they sat at breakfast. He dressed quickly and ran downstairs. He was bursting with excitement.

His father stood on the patio, smoking his pipe; the blue smoke circled lazily above in the sunlight. When Eric quietly came up behind him, he turned around

and said, "Morning, son. Your tie is crooked." Nothing more! His mother straightened his tie and set a bowl of corn flakes down at his place. His brothers drank their coffee and read the newspaper. Every so often, when Theo turned a page he made a face at Eric, but this, too, was just like every other day. Somewhat insulted, Eric ate his breakfast, keeping a close eye on the dining room door. But not a single ant crossed the threshold. A fly sat there for a moment, but since Eric had definitely not invited him, he just kept eating silently.

As soon as his lunchbox was ready, Eric left for school. He felt very strange. All the houses were exactly the same, and no one seemed to take any particular notice of him. At school, too, nothing had changed. Willy Martin sat a few seats ahead of him in the same place as before, and when the bell rang, he turned around and asked Eric if he had also done the mayflies. No, he hadn't.

Eric didn't do too well on the test. Miss Gastworthy had drawn a red line through a number of his answers, with the words "nonsense" and "ridiculous" in the margin. Eric's answer to the question, "Do the wasps belong to the group of useful insects?" was "That is very possible, but they'll bore you to death if you visit them." Here Miss Gastworthy had written in big, red letters: "Are you ill? What is the matter with you? Come see me after class!"

Eric remained behind when everyone else left at the end of the schoolday. His answers to Miss Gastworthy's questions were so bizarre that there was nothing left for her to do but sharpen the point on her red pencil and write a note to Eric's mother, saying that this must not continue and a lot of work needed to be done.

"His mayflies in particular are extremely weak, and as far as the wasps and the ants are concerned, his ideas are completely at variance with everything that Solm has written. In connection with the upcoming school inspection, I felt it unjust not to inform you of the state of affairs. I trust that something can and will be done to rectify this situation."

It was indeed difficult to be the subject of such a letter after one had spent a whole month in the insect world, where one had only to open one's mouth to amaze all listeners with one's knowledge—but Eric remained silent. He had to go to bed an hour early that evening, and there he remained, patiently waiting to shrink again and then never, never to come back to this unappreciative world. Those were Eric's thoughts, but human expectations are not always fulfilled. The miracle never happened again—not that evening, nor the following evening, nor any of the evenings to come.

That was long, long ago; so long ago that if Eric were now asked about it, he would probably just smile and stare out the window. That's how it goes with growing up. Because Eric is now indeed grown up. He could himself even be the father of a little Eric.

He did not become a famous entomologist, as one might have expected. But one peculiar consequence of that evening does remain: sometimes, in the company of other people, he cannot stop himself from thinking of certain insects. One time it is the van Thinwings; another time, the bumblebees; yet another, the worms or the gravediggers. Occasionally he even runs into a spider. He sees quite a few snails, and the ants are becoming more common every day. It's a strange feeling for someone who had once been in the land of the insects.

And so ends our story of Eric Pinksterblom. Godspeed to all, keep your eye on the frame, and try not to become overly fond of honey.